g Stilettos
Sparkling Stars
Sparkling Souls

Sparkling Souls

ISBN # 978-1-7868-61924

Interior text design by Claire Siemaszkiewicz

Totally Bound Publishing

Published in 2017 by Totally Bound Publishing, United Kingdom.

Totally Bound Publishing is a subsidiary of Totally Entwined Group Limited.

Sparkling

SPARKLING SOULS

JESS WRIGHT

Dedication

I am dedicating this book to my Nan. Nanny Pat. We miss you every second of every day. I know you are still there watching over and probably laughing with Grandad. Everything I do I think of you and try to make you happy. The television randomly switching off, the robins Mum always sees in the garden and the endless amounts of white feathers that come my way are all signification that you are with us always. I particularly loved the one I found in between my phone and phone case…very clever even from you, Nan! You were a light in everyone's life and I will love you forever. I'm looking after Mummy like you asked me to.

My angel always, Jess xx

1

Megan

Megan Winter stared at the man standing before her. His face, once so familiar, had become a distant memory, and his endearment, honey-pie, rang uncomfortably in her ears.

He grinned and tipped his head, swiping his tongue over his bottom lip as he did so.

"What…what are you doing here?" she asked, removing her hand from her mouth then clutching the doorframe.

"Jesus, girl, you look like you've seen a ghost. It's only me." He held his palms out. "Nothing to worry about."

She didn't believe him. The last time she'd seen Dylan, he'd oozed menace. His eyes had flashed with determination to get her back and a certain mad obsessiveness had lurked in their depths.

She took a step backwards but collided with a solid chest.

James.

He wrapped his arm around her waist and pulled her near. His chin pressed her temple and his breath warmed her skin.

Gripping his forearm, glad of his strength, she stared steadily at Dylan.

His eyes widened as he looked at James. "You," he said.

"Hey, mate, what are you doing here?" James' voice was light and breezy.

A weird sensation rolled around Megan. It was almost as if James knew Dylan.

But he didn't.

He couldn't.

James released Megan and held out his hand.

Dylan shook it. It seemed that it was now his turn to go pale. "But in the bar…"

"Yeah, you said…" James spoke slowly, as though pieces of a jigsaw were falling into place. "That you'd come to LA to get your girl back."

James tensed.

"Oh, love a duck, look who it isn't." Brendon appeared on Megan's other side, his voice high and skittish. "Dylan Dunkin-Buckshaw, what the devil are you doing in LA?" He paused and turned his head back the way he'd just come. "Hey, Georgie, get your sassy arse out here. Come see who it is."

"Quite the party you've got going on," Dylan said, wrinkling his nose. "You have your entire cavalry here, Megan."

"Actually, it was a bit of a party." Megan tried to keep the shake from her voice.

"And unless I am sorely mistaken, we didn't send you an invite," Brendon added huffily.

Dylan retreated a step down the path. He shoved his hands into the pockets of his trousers and hunched his shoulders.

He was outnumbered. The bravado had left him. That menacing aura he projected whenever Megan was alone with him wasn't so evident now.

"Dylan!" Georgie gasped. "Why are you here?"

He didn't answer. Instead, he stared at Megan for a few seconds then gazed down at his feet.

Suddenly Megan felt bad. Dylan wasn't the one for her, she knew that now with every fibre in her soul. That fact would never change. He was controlling and delusional and occasionally just plain old nasty. But that didn't mean she wanted him to be unhappy, or never find a person to spend his life with. She just didn't want it to be her. No way.

"Are you okay, Megan?" James asked, pulling her close again.

She nodded, despite the deluge of conflicting emotions she was experiencing. "Dylan. Why don't you come in?"

He peeked back up at her, hope in his expression.

"Are you off your trolley?" Brendon gasped.

"No." She turned to Brendon. "Dylan has come all this way—clearly it isn't over for him even though it is for me." She tilted her chin, took a deep breath and looked at Dylan again. "The least I can do is hear him out."

"Thank you," Dylan said, straightening slightly.

Megan leaned into James a little more, his body heat comforting. "As long as you know this, Dylan, I'm not going to be walking out of here with you, or putting on any rings you've got secreted away in your pockets." She tried to use her sternest voice.

Dylan glanced between Megan and James. "Yeah, I get that now."

"Bloody Nora," Brendon said. "I need a drink. Come on, Georgie, let's make it a stiff one."

"A big stiff one." Georgie rolled her eyes.

Brendon laughed. "The bigger the better."

"Are you sure about this?" James asked Megan quietly.

"Yes." Megan nodded. "I owe him this." She gazed up at James, at his kind eyes and his handsome face. As much as she knew Dylan wasn't the one for her, she knew James was. He was everything she needed in a man—considerate, tough, intelligent, loyal and, most of all, he made her feel like she was the most important thing in his life, as if her happiness were his priority. And in return, for her, seeing him smile, seeing James happy, was what she wanted most.

"Okay." He gave her a squeeze. "I won't be far away."

"You don't need to worry," Dylan said. "I'm not here to cause trouble."

"You're not?" Megan asked.

He huffed. "Well, maybe I was ready to fight to get you back, but that's changed."

"What's changed?" James asked, a hint of menace in his tone.

"You," Dylan said, nodding at James. "What you said in the First Base bar, about having found a special someone."

"I have. She's very special." James tucked a lock of hair behind Megan's ear.

It was a small gesture but it screamed possessiveness. Stay away. She's mine. Megan didn't mind it in the least. Had the shoe been on the other foot, a woman from James' past showing up, she'd have been staking her claim on her man big time.

"What happened at First Base bar?" she asked.

James shrugged. "We bumped into each other."

"Obviously without knowing who we were talking to," Dylan added. "We talked about you."

Megan shook her head. Fate had put her life on a weird track lately. "Why don't you come through, Dylan? We can talk out the back. In the courtyard."

Dylan nodded again. "Okay."

James seemed reluctant to let her go, but he did and stood stock still as Dylan walked into the house and followed Megan through the hallway to the kitchen.

She paused and filled two glasses with iced water, then stepped into the shade of the neat walled back garden. Several butterflies hovered around the mass of flowers that tumbled over the fence and for a moment she stared at them, wondering at how simple their lives were compared to hers.

Dylan's presence behind her created a heavy sadness in her gut. Why had he bothered to come all this way? Made such a long journey just to go over the same old ground? She'd always known he was stubborn, but this was a new level.

At least the anger seemed to have gone from him.

Unless that was all an act for her friends.

Feeling suddenly vulnerable in the small quiet space, and alone with the man who'd caused her to flee London, she turned.

Dylan dragged out a patio chair from under the table, the

legs scraping on the paving slabs covering the ground. He sat.

A flash of movement in the kitchen window caught her attention.

James.

He was keeping an eye on things.

Feeling braver, she set the two drinks on the table and sat opposite the man she'd walked down the aisle to marry… except she hadn't, she'd jilted him at the altar.

"Thanks," he said, pulling his drink closer.

Somehow he looked smaller than he used to.

He retrieved his shades from where he'd poked them into the neck of his T-shirt and laid them on the table. He then took off his peaked cap and rubbed his hand over his hair.

"I don't understand what you're doing here," Megan said, running her fingers over the condensation covering her glass of water. "I thought you understood that we were over."

"Have you ever been in love, Megan? I mean, really and truly in heart-stopping, soul-wrenching love?"

"Is that a trick question?" She frowned.

"No. Not at all."

"I thought I was in love with you," she said quietly.

"You only thought…"

"Yes, but now…" She paused. "Now I think I was in love with the idea of being in love, getting married, having the happily ever after. I don't know if what I felt came from here." She pressed her hand over her chest.

He nodded.

"And I'm so, so sorry I didn't realise that until the last minute."

"We've gone past apologies," he said, a resigned expression crossing his face.

"But I will always be sorry for what happened that day in church, it was a cruel thing to do."

He took a sip of his water then smiled a little ruefully. "It was, but if it helps, you're forgiven."

Megan remained silent.

A plane overhead roared past.

"But I was in heart-stopping, soul-wrenching love with you," he said when the noise had faded.

"But were you?" She shook her head. "Were you really?"

"Yes, of course."

"But you..." She hesitated. "Looking back, I seemed to annoy you."

"Annoy me?"

"Yes. Most of the time I wasn't wearing the right thing, saying the right thing, and you didn't like my red lipstick." Automatically she touched her lips, which were of course coated in her favourite MAC colour. "Everything about me seemed to irritate you," she went on. "I don't think I made you happy, Dylan, not really. You were always trying to change me."

"Is that how I made you feel? Like you were never right?"

She nodded, a balloon of emotion swelling in her chest. "Yes. I spent a lot of my time managing your moods, your..." To hell with it, she'd just say it. Dylan couldn't hurt her anymore and it might just be for his own good. "Managing your temper."

He balled his fists on the table.

Megan glanced at the kitchen window. She could just make out James' outline. He was standing very still and appeared to have his attention set entirely on her and Dylan.

That made her feel a whole lot better.

"For the record, I thought, and still do think, you're perfect," Dylan said.

"Can I give you a bit of advice then?" Megan stared straight at him.

"Go for it." He blinked slowly, as though not really wanting to hear what was going to be said.

"Next time you're dating, tell her you think she's perfect. Let her wear and eat and do what she wants, because you'll soon find it's what you want, too." She paused. "And it's what attracted you to her in the first place."

"Next time." He huffed. "There was only you, Megan. I'm done with this whole love game."

"Don't be ridiculous." She held out her hands, palms to the sky. "You're young, you've got your whole life ahead of you. There's someone for everyone, you know."

"And I guess you've found that someone." He jerked his thumb over his shoulder, towards the kitchen.

Megan rested back in the chair and again looked at James' silhouette. "Yes. I have."

"As I said before when I met him, in the bar earlier," Dylan said, picking up his shades and fiddling with the arms. "We got chatting…about you."

Megan was quiet, waiting for him to continue.

"Of course I had no idea he was the new man in my fiancée's life, your name was never mentioned."

"Ex-fiancée."

"Er, yes, sorry, ex, of course." He shrugged. "Anyway, he said that he'd met a special lady who made it worth coming home to at the end of the day. Someone he was in love with."

"James said that? To you?" Megan wanted to believe it, really she did. It made it all seem so much more real, more permanent between her and James if he was talking about her like that to other people. And what he'd said, it was the way she felt about him, too.

Dylan was studying her. "He also said that this woman he was in love with was beautiful inside and out, talented, fun, and drove him crazy and made him complete."

She had a sip of water then kept hold of her cool glass as it rested on the table.

He reached out and captured her hand, trapping it between both of his. "I'd come to LA to fight for you, to try and persuade you to come back to me. I was prepared to do anything, try whatever tactic worked."

"I'm not coming back to you." It was strange to have him touch her. Familiar yet alien. Comfortable but not.

The back door opened. James stood there, his eyes

narrowed and his arms crossed over his chest.

A flutter of apprehension took flight in her belly. She knew James didn't take kindly to other men thinking she was theirs—hell, the last guy who had had ended up with a black eye. Being an A-list Hollywood actor hadn't made a jot of difference.

Dylan didn't appear to notice James. "I know that you'll never be mine again. I didn't know that, not for a long time. I don't know if I was blind or in denial. Or if hope was the strongest emotion I had to hold on to. Plus…" He shook his head. "No one has ever dumped me before, Megan."

She didn't reply.

"That bloke in there." He gave a backwards nod.

"James."

"Yeah, James. He really bloody loves you, you know that?"

Megan swallowed and again glanced at James.

"If I thought," Dylan went on, "for one moment that he didn't, that he'd not treat you right, then I wouldn't give up on you." He released her hand and reached for his cap, slapping it on his head. "You only deserve the best, Megan. You really do."

"I think that's true of us all."

"Maybe, but you…well, you're special."

"I want you to find someone, Dylan, the way I have."

"Maybe I will, maybe I won't." He picked up his water and drank it in several large gulps, the way he did with beer. When he'd finished, he set it down and stood.

Megan got to her feet. "What will you do now? In LA?"

"I've got a return flight in a week. The old me thought that would be as long as I needed to win you back." He shook his head. "Now, I think I'll hire a car and do some exploring, maybe get myself to Vegas."

"Sounds fun."

James stepped into the courtyard and over to Megan. His upper arm brushed hers. "All okay?"

"Yeah." Dylan slipped on his shades. "I'm just leaving."

He gave James' shoulder a friendly whack. "So you don't need to worry about me anymore, unless, that is, you upset Megan. She deserves the best, you know."

"I do know, and I have no intention of upsetting her." James was still tense.

Megan knew he wasn't enjoying this whole situation.

"Good," Dylan said, "because if you do, you'll have me to deal with." He reached for Megan's hand, lifted it to his lips and swept a kiss over her knuckles. "Take care, and good luck, you know, with the shoes and all that."

"Thanks, Dylan. You take care, too."

He released her hand. "I'll show myself out."

Megan watched him disappear into the kitchen then listened as his footsteps faded and the front door slammed, the breeze catching it. She blew out a long, low breath as stress slipped from her body.

"Do you think that's the last we'll hear from him?" James asked, winding his arms around her waist and pulling her close.

She slotted her hands behind his neck and looked up at him. "I hope so. He's been so persistent and amazingly stubborn, but I think he's got the message." She smiled. "Whatever you said to him in that bar worked."

James rolled his eyes. "What are the chances, eh? Of me talking to a complete stranger about how in love with you I am and it turns out to be your ex."

Megan smiled as warmth spread through her. Hearing James say he loved her would never get old, never get boring. Spoken by him, in his confident, deep voice, it was the sweetest thing she'd ever heard.

She reached up and kissed him, losing herself in the man who had become her world.

"Megan, Megan. Has Dylan gone?" Georgie's voice filled the courtyard.

"Oh, for the love of God, will you two get a room," Brendon said with an exasperated sigh.

Megan tore herself from James and turned to her friends.

"Yes, he's gone, and this time I think that's it, for good."

"You don't think he'll show up again?" Georgie asked.

"Sure he will," Brendon said. "He's like eating a rotten egg that keeps generating bad smells over and over. Coming back to haunt you when you least expect it."

"Ick, when have you ever eaten a rotten egg?" Georgie asked, grimacing at Brendon.

"Well, I haven't, but I'd imagine the smells would be pretty gross." He shrugged.

Megan smiled, enjoying the fact that Dylan had been and gone without incident. Plus he had seemed to get that they were over this time. "I think this really is the last we'll see of him, unless we head to Vegas over the next week."

"Vegas?" Zane said, appearing at Brendon's side.

Brendon slipped his arm around his new boyfriend. Apparently the 'get a room' rule didn't apply to them. "You want to go to Vegas?"

"With you, anytime." Zane shrugged. "Except this week. We have to get Megan ready for The Paul Piper Show on Friday."

A tumble of nerves hit Megan at the mention of the chat show. She had a lot of things to put straight with the nation's media, not least telling the world she wasn't with Hollywood actor Tate Simmons, despite having been on his arm at an award ceremony the previous week. And that was before she gave her fashion brand, Winter Shoes, a good plug.

Brendon slapped his palm to his forehead. "Yes, there's that, and I'm expecting a delivery of more shoes for LA Hype."

"Oh, including Greta Breen's order?"

"Yes, and when Greta wears them to the Oscars they're going to be flying off the shelves, so we'll need a good supply."

"So exciting." Zane grinned broadly.

"And, we're forgetting something else." Georgie whipped a tape measure from her pocket. "I need measurements, from you" — she flicked the end of the tape at Brendon, then at Megan — "and you."

"What for?" Megan asked, frowning.

Georgie tutted. "For my wedding, of course. It's only a matter of weeks away and you're not going to be in London for fittings."

A pinch of shame nipped at Megan's conscience.

Of course, my best friend's wedding.

She'd been so wrapped up in her own world — her business just taking off and a love she'd only just allowed herself to fall into — that she'd almost forgotten the most important thing going on in Georgie's life.

"Absolutely," she said, grinning. "Let's get to it." She stepped back from James and held out her arms. "Measure away."

2

Megan woke before James and was content to stay relaxed and tranquil in his arms.

The sounds of the waves filtered towards her through a small open window, the breeze catching the sheer white curtains at the French doors and causing them to flutter. She stared at the picture on the wall opposite. It was of the ocean, a great curling wave cresting, just about to crash down. For a moment, she thought she could smell the painting, then she remembered that this close to the Pacific, the breezy air in the house was always briny.

All of the pictures James had in his home—or rather, her home now, for that was how he'd told her to think of it—were of nature. He had the Grand Canyon in the living room, a picture of Everest in the kitchen and a large mural of a rainforest in the study area.

He stirred and slid his hand over her stomach, tugging her nearer.

She smiled then turned to face him, inhaling the scent of his bed-warm skin and knowing that it was her most favourite smell of all. Nothing else compared.

"Mmm, morning," he said, kissing the top of her head.

She dragged him closer still. "Morning. What time is it?"

He shifted to look at the bedside clock. "Nearly nine."

"What time is Rue expecting us?"

"It starts at lunchtime, so we've got a few hours."

"Good." Megan wasn't in the mood for rushing, even though she'd been looking forward to an afternoon on Rue's fancy yacht for the last few days. If she were honest, it had been one of the things that had kept her going.

She'd been so sad to see Georgie leave for the UK, but had known it was always going to happen. Georgie's fiancé, Tom, was in London, as was her business and her home. The fact that she'd managed a trip to LA at all was nothing short of a miracle, considering all that was going on. Georgie was a 'live life in the fast lane' kind of girl, but travelling half way around the world for a shoe launch on Rodeo Drive was a big ask, even if it had been Megan's birthday.

"You okay?" James asked.

"Yes, fine."

"Thinking about Georgie?"

She smiled. "You know me well, but actually now I'm thinking about a shower and then maybe eggs for breakfast."

"I think that can be arranged." He pushed back the covers and stood.

He walked naked to the window and, obviously knowing he had privacy from the beach because of the height of the house, he opened the French doors and stared out to sea.

Megan looked at him as the curtains billowed into the room on the breeze. She still had to pinch herself sometimes to make sure it was true. This gorgeous man who was proud and loving, and really did have the cutest bum she'd ever seen, was all hers.

Smiling, she stretched out her spine, curled her toes, clenched her fists, then blew out a breath. It was time to make a move and get going for the day.

She slipped from the bed then headed into the large en suite. She switched on the shower and, while the water heated, she brushed her teeth. Soon steam swirled around the room and after checking the temperature, she stepped in. As she held her face to the water and let the stream soak her hair, strong arms wrapped around her waist.

"Want some company?" James asked, pressing a kiss to her neck and his body against hers.

"If your shampooing skills are up to scratch," she said, smiling.

"I think you'll find I have many skills that I could put to use in here."

She giggled and reached for the shampoo. "Well, start with this one."

"Yes, Miss."

The scent of lavender filled the air as he began to massage her scalp, working the suds into a lather and leaving no section of her hair untouched.

Megan sighed. Bliss. What a way to start the day.

When he seemed satisfied the job was done, he tugged her back under the stream of water and carefully rinsed the shampoo away, making sure it didn't wash over her eyes. He then repeated the same routine with conditioner.

"How's that?" he asked, smoothing the strands into a long, wet ponytail that hung down her back.

"I think you missed your vocation."

He chuckled. "As a hairdresser?"

"Yes."

"Trouble is, I only want to wash your hair and to be honest…"

"What?"

"I prefer to do it naked." Once again he wrapped his arms around her waist. "Might cause trouble with some clients."

Smiling, she spun around. "So about these other skills?"

He raised his eyebrows. "Ah, them…"

"Yes, them. Are you going to show me?"

He bit on his bottom lip, as though holding in a grin.

"James." She frowned. He was being a tease, and right now, she just needed to be as close to him as possible. Naked and in the shower wasn't enough. She wanted more.

She wanted everything he had to give.

"You really want me to show you?"

"Yes, you know I do."

He lowered his head and kissed her. A hot, hungry kiss that tasted of the same toothpaste she'd just used. His tongue stroked hers.

She gripped his shoulders—hard and solid. She didn't want to ever let him go. And she wouldn't, not for anything. They were together now, end of story.

Megan and James.

He slid his hands down her back, then lower still.

She gasped as he suddenly lifted her into the air and pressed her shoulders to the cool wall tiles.

"James," she said, wrapping her legs around his waist.

"If my day started with you in my arms, every day, for the rest of my life, I'd be a happy man," he said.

"And in your shower?" She looked into his dark eyes. His lashes were wet and had stuck together in tiny triangles.

"That works, too." He adjusted the angle of her hips and positioned himself.

She held her breath. Locked her hands behind his neck.

He kissed her once more and eased in, his chest rubbing hers.

They began to move against each other. Megan's breaths turned to short, sharp pants. He was so damn good at hitting the spot, making it just right for her.

Still the water descended, blasting down on them. But Megan barely noticed the rivulets pouring over their bodies. Now it was all about pleasure, about reaching that cresting wave of ecstasy together.

On and on, James took them towards it.

Soon she was clutching at his hair, trembling, her need growing to the point it was going to overspill.

"Megan," he gasped.

"Oh, James, don't stop…" she said.

"I won't." He upped the tempo.

She toppled into ecstasy.

He joined her, holding her close as he groaned long and low, the sound echoing around the cubicle and swirling with the steam.

Megan shut her eyes, savouring the moment of absolute satisfaction. In James' arms, like this, joined, she only wanted to be here. Their closeness was like nothing else she'd ever experienced. It wasn't just their bodies—it was their minds, their emotions, their souls. They were tangled now, their lives running parallel. She didn't imagine anything would ever or could ever change the way she felt about him right at this minute. His love was burned into her heart—it was in every breath she took and every thought she had.

"That was an energetic start to what is supposed to be a relaxing day," James said breathlessly.

"I'm not complaining."

"Me neither." He kissed her then lowered her feet to the floor. "Maybe I'll have to offer my shampooing services more often."

She giggled. "It certainly comes with extras."

A few hours later they were heading towards Newport Beach in James' car.

He had the roof down, and at first Megan worried about her hair and makeup, but then she realised they'd soon be speeding out into the ocean and she'd be at one with the elements anyway.

She'd opted for a short white dress that had thin straps and pale yellow daisies embroidered onto it. Teamed with a thin cashmere shawl—in case the breeze was cooler out at sea—and flat sandals from her latest range, she was all set for her day on deck.

It took a few minutes to find a parking space at the marina, but once they had they were soon walking past the many luxury yachts that called Newport home.

"Hey, James. There you are," a portly man in shorts and a striped shirt called as he waved at them. He wore a navy hat with a white brim.

"That's Rue," James said, keeping a firm hold of her hand.

"Ah, so now I get to meet your boss?"

"Yeah."

Megan studied Rue as he walked towards them. James wasn't the sort of person she could visualise anyone bossing around. He did his own thing. And if for some reason he was doing something he didn't want to, it was pretty obvious—like the Baywatch-style documentary he'd had dropped on him recently. He'd thought it frivolous and crass, not his sort of thing at all. James was happiest making documentaries that exposed corruption, highlighted injustice, changed the world. And heck, he was pretty damn good at it. He'd just won a major industry award for his work on *Poor Choices,* which concentrated on the struggle poverty-ridden families in the western world had to face.

"I'm glad you're here, we're all set to leave," Rue said, grinning.

"Sorry, are we late?" James asked, glancing at his watch.

"No, you're bang on time, but I wouldn't blame you if you were late with such a beautiful distraction." Rue turned to Megan. "It's a pleasure to meet you, Miss Winter."

"Megan, please." She took his offered hand.

"Megan." Rue smiled. "Diane is dying to meet you. She's a complete fashionista and just desperate to hear all about your shoe designs. Apparently, she bought a pair when she was on Rodeo Drive last week." He rolled his eyes. "Not that she's allowed to wear them today, flat shoes only on *Black Rose*. A quarter-of-a-million-dollar deck refurbishment put paid to stilettoes."

"Oh, yes, of course." Megan was doubly glad she'd worn flats.

"Come, come, this way." Rue gave James a friendly slap on his arm then marched them past a row of yachts.

There was one black boat set amongst the line of shiny white ones. Megan guessed straight away that it was Black Rose. Low and sleek, it had a thin red stripe around it and, as they drew closer, she could see the accessories were red, too—plush leather seating, red curtains at the darkened windows and even staff with red silk shirts.

"Looks amazing," James said.

"Ah, I forget, you haven't been on this one before, have you, James?"

"No, the old one, what was it…? *Black Diamond.*"

"You have a good memory." Rue nodded and stopped before a red-carpeted gangplank that had a roped handrail.

"And be prepared to be impressed. This baby is an extra fifty square feet and has considerably more horsepower."

"I'm already impressed," Megan said, a roll of excitement catching in her belly. *A day on this amazing boat? How exciting. How different to my life in London. This I could get used to.*

Rue indicated for Megan to head onto the boat first. As she stepped aboard, she was offered a glass of champagne, which she took.

James joined her and as they clinked glasses with Rue, a pretty woman with brown bobbed hair approached them.

"James," she said, "how wonderful to see you."

He smiled and pressed a kiss to her cheek. "Diane, you're looking well."

"Thank you." She patted her hair and swiped her tongue over her lips, which were coated in baby-pink lipstick. "And you must be Megan."

"Yes, hello."

"I'm so pleased you could make it," Diane said. "You've been quite the talk of the town, what with schmoozing with Tate Simmons at the ceremony."

"Well I wasn't really with him. I mean, I went with him but we soon parted company." She saw James' fingers tighten on the stem of his glass. The sooner this stupid rumour about her and Tate being in a relationship was quashed the better.

"Handsome man, though, don't you think?" Diane said.

"I guess he has the looks Hollywood wants." She moved a little closer to James and pressed her hand against the small of his back. "But he doesn't have anything I want."

"Oh?" Diane raised her perfectly arched eyebrows. "I sense gossip."

"No gossip." Megan shrugged, hoping to deflect Diane's interest. "He's just not the one for me."

"Which is just as well," Rue cut in. "As it seems our James has got a twinkle in his eye for you."

"A very handsome couple you make, too," Diane said. "And, Megan, you simply must give me all the lowdown on Winter Shoes. I bought myself a pair from this season's heeled range. They're perfectly divine, like walking on air, and so versatile. I just know they're going to be a hit."

"Thank you." Megan smiled. "I'll happily chat shoes all day."

Diane's attention was suddenly caught by someone on her right. "There's Lavinia Heat. If I don't introduce you, Megan, it would be a crime."

"Lavinia Heat," Megan repeated. She knew the name. Lavinia had her own chat show. It was on late at night and was a round-up of what the stars had been wearing all week. It was cheeky, a lot of fun and bang on when it came to trend spotting.

"You ladies go ahead. I've actually got news for James." Rue nodded.

"You have?" James said, raising his eyebrows.

"Yes, the board have looked at your proposal."

"Oh, okay." James pulled in a deep breath.

"Come, this way," Diane said, hooking her hand beneath Megan's elbow. "Lavinia is going to adore you, what with your cute little English accent and your pretty smile."

"Well…okay, thanks." Megan glanced at James, but he was already huddling close to Rue as their conversation quietened and appeared to turn serious. She hoped it wasn't bad news about his proposal. She knew he'd been counting the days until he got a decision on whether or not he could go ahead with his next documentary.

Though truth be told, she'd rather he picked something a little closer to home than Central America, and certainly something a bit safer than exposing drug gangs.

"Don't worry, James won't go far," Diane said.

"What do you mean?" Did Diane know something? Had the proposal been turned down?

"Well, he can't, can he?" She chuckled. "Anchor's up now, we're all on here for the day, unless anyone decides to take a dunking, that is, and jump overboard."

As they walked towards Lavinia, who was lounging on

one of the red sofas, having her champagne flute topped up, Megan noticed that the boat was now moving. It sliced through the water, and beneath her feet, the soft vibrations of the engine rumbled upwards. "Where are we going?"

"Oh, just down the coast a few miles. Away from the madness that is LA. Rue is planning a little black jack and poker to raise some cash for the charity his sister set up last year. It's all good fun though, just an excuse to use the boat with close friends."

Close friends and some of the biggest names in the film and TV industry, Megan thought as another familiar face smiled her way. A newsreader, if she remembered rightly, from CNN.

"Lavinia, darling," Diane said, wafting her drink in the air. "You must meet Megan Winter, it's quite a coup to have her on board. Everyone, and I mean everyone, is talking about her shoe range, fresh from London. And let me tell you, it's utterly fabulous."

"Ah, fresh blood from London?" Lavinia smiled wickedly and her eyes twinkled as she took in Megan.

Megan had the urge to shrink backwards. The woman was witchy looking, with thick powder on her cheeks and a black swimsuit beneath a loose and diaphanous cover-up. But instead Megan stood tall and smiled politely. "It's lovely to meet you."

"And I you. Sit, sit, dear, tell me all about it."

Megan sat on the warm leather and crossed her legs. The breeze was picking up a little as the speed of the boat increased and she was glad of its cool fingers stroking her skin.

"So, dear, I know just about everyone in this crazy town, but you, you're new." Lavinia sat back and set her attention on Megan. "Which is always a treat, so why don't you tell me all about yourself and that hunk you stepped on board with?"

3

Megan had never met anyone quite like Lavinia Heat. Sure, she'd seen her on television, even caught the odd interview she'd given, but in 'real' life, well, she was even more exuberant. It also seemed she had no filter for what she said, which of course was likely the reason she was so successful as a chat show host. She spoke to shock, her wit was razor-sharp and her inquisitive mind knew no bounds.

As the land grew smaller and a beaty tune came from the interior of the boat, where more people stood about talking, Megan was thoroughly grilled with Diane watching on.

"And which shop did you say the launch was in?" Lavinia asked, popping a smoked salmon blini into her mouth.

"LA Hype. They've been very kind to me."

"Nonsense, they're lucky to have you, if, as you say, Greta Breen is wearing you to the Oscars."

"Well…yes, she is."

"And they know they're on to a good thing. They'll be seeing dollar signs, you mark my words, little one."

Little one?

"And what about these?" Lavinia nodded at Megan's sandals. "Are they yours?"

"Of course. They're from my new summer beach range."

"Selling?"

"I'm delighted to say yes, they are."

"And who's worn them?"

"I'm not sure about these particular ones." Megan drained the last of her champagne. Immediately a member of the catering staff refilled her glass. "Thank you."

"From this range, I do believe Nancy Day has just been spotted out in them." Diane nodded seriously.

"Oh, has she now?" Lavinia tapped her chin as though

storing that piece of information away.

"And Amanda Rush is already a mad Winter Shoes fan," Diane added.

"Yes, she's wearing my pale pink, lace-overlay design to the Golden Globes," Megan added.

"Your design?" For the first time Lavinia looked impressed.

"Yes, apparently she's thrilled with them—they'll go perfectly with her outfit."

"Well, well, you do have connections in all the right places." Lavinia held her up empty glass and it was at once refilled. "Amanda Rush has faultless taste. I'm impressed, Megan Winter."

Megan sipped her champagne. She hadn't expected to feel such a rush of pleasure at Lavinia's words. But she did. This woman could make or break a newbie in the LA fashion world and it seemed she liked her.

"Mmm..." Lavinia was studying Megan and tapping her chin again.

"What?" Megan asked hesitantly. She wished James was with her. *Where is he?*

"Have you ever done TV?" Lavinia asked.

"TV?" Megan repeated. "What do you mean?"

"You know what I mean. Have you ever been on TV? Talked to the nation about Winter Shoes?"

"Actually, I have. Back in London I stepped in a few times on *Ralph and Jayne.*"

She wrinkled her nose. "*Ralph and Jayne?* What's that?"

"It's a daytime chat show. They talk about everything from eating disorders to recipes to fashion. They needed someone to talk shoes, they asked me." Megan shrugged as though it were nothing, but truth be told she'd been ecstatic and nervous in equal quantities—it had been Brendon who'd encouraged her to do it.

"And how'd you get on in front of a camera?"

"Fine, well..." She smiled broadly. "They asked me back, so I guess that says something."

"I'm sure they did ask you back, honey." She leaned closer, so close her heavily spiced perfume tickled Megan's nose. "How'd you fancy coming on my show? I do a guest spot each month."

"Your show?"

"Yep, it's mine. I can ask who I want, and you, little one, I want."

"You do?" Megan's head was swimming. Had she heard Lavinia right?

"Yes, we're bitchy when we see something that reminds us of vomit, and yes, we'll slate someone if they think less is more when really they've got more on show than should be. But we tell it how it is, we say what everyone else is thinking but is too scared to."

"Well, I've seen it, your show, obviously. Since I've been in LA," Megan said.

"And did you like it?"

Megan didn't think that had really been a question. "Of course. It's a firm favourite."

"So we're all set. This Friday you can be my special guest—I've got an unexpected slot. Like it and you can come back. I've been searching for a shoe guru for years. You're just the little English poppet I've been needing to come along."

"I'm flattered." Megan thought of the exposure for her brand being on Lavinia Heats It Up would bring. Brendon would likely cry with excitement.

"So it's a yes?" Lavinia held up her glass, an expectant expression in her eyes.

"Yes…oh…no." Megan's heart sank. "I can't, not this Friday."

"And why's that? Is studly over there taking you for dinner?" She nodded over Megan's shoulder in the direction of James. "Surely you can rearrange."

"No, nothing like that. I'm on The Paul Piper Show."

"Paul Piper!" Lavinia screeched. "That good for nothing, low life, gossip monger. Why are you going on his show?"

Megan was slightly alarmed by Lavinia's reaction and clear dislike of Paul Piper. "I said I would." And she couldn't change it, she was committed. In fact, she was looking forward to it, to using the opportunity to tell the world that she was nothing to do with Tate Simmons. It was ridiculous that Brendon had needed to fend off press calls asking when she was marrying the Hollywood star. Why the hell would she marry Tate Simmons when she was in love with James Carter? Not to mention she strongly suspected Tate Simmons was still in love with his rock star ex-girlfriend and had used Megan to make her jealous.

Lavinia rolled her eyes and tutted.

"But what about another time?" Diane suggested, flapping her hand at a waiter and indicating Lavinia's once again empty glass.

It was hastily filled.

"Mmm, four weeks from now?" Lavinia suggested.

"That would work for me," Megan said, hating the thought of losing the opportunity to sit in front of the nation and talk shoes. "You know, if that's suitable for your schedule." She'd make damn sure it worked for hers.

Lavinia tipped her chin in the air and shook her dark, curled hair over her shoulders, the wind helping it on its way. "It would be glorious." She grinned suddenly and chinked glasses with Megan. "Seems as if we have ourselves a date on national TV."

Relief swamped Megan. Thank goodness. Brendon would have flipped his lid if she'd blown it. "Great. I'm looking forward to it."

"Just be prepared for the heat." Lavinia cackled and Diane joined in.

What have I let myself in for?

"Hey, baby, how are you doing?"

James stood before her, his hair being tousled by the wind.

"I'm fine."

"More than fine, she's going to be my guest and bring her

fancy shoes with her," Lavinia said, standing. She pressed her hand over her lips, supressing a hiccup.

"A guest?" James raised his eyebrows.

"Yes, on *Lavinia Heats It Up*." Megan smiled.

James appeared slightly bemused.

Megan knew why. He'd never heard of the show. And why would he? He was sweet and did a good job of showing interest in her shoe designs, but he was hardly a follower of fashion himself, and what the Hollywood stars wore probably wasn't—or ever would be—on his radar.

"That sounds great," he said, smiling.

"She's quite a cutie, and clearly has a brain." Lavinia waved her hand in Megan's direction. "Keep hold of her."

"I intend to."

A big hiccup escaped Lavinia. "I think I'll pay the little girls' room a visit."

"Okay, I'll show you the way." Diane slipped her hand around Lavinia's waist and steered her towards the interior of the boat.

"You okay?" James asked, sitting next to Megan.

"Fine." She smiled.

"Want to get out of the sun?" He nodded at the doors, which were wide open and offered the sanctuary of the living area.

"No, I'm loving it out here. The sound of the waves, the heat mixed with the breeze, it's perfect."

"You're perfect." He pressed a kiss to her cheek.

"I know it doesn't mean much to you," Megan said, "but Lavinia's show is watched by millions. A guest spot on there, chatting fashion and giving my brand a plug, is the sort of advertisement money can't buy."

"Well, it's better than the advertisement of going out with a Hollywood A-lister."

She dug him in the ribs. "But I'm not, am I? Unless you count yourself a Hollywood A-lister."

"You know I don't." He propped his forearms on his thighs and leant forwards, then peered at his feet.

"Hey, it's okay. I'll put paid to the Tate rumour soon." She rested her hand on his back and rubbed. "It will be dead and buried before the week is out. As soon as I've been on The Paul Piper Show."

"I know."

"So…what's up?" She paused. "What did Rue say about your proposal?"

He didn't answer.

"James?"

"I got it."

"You did." She forced herself to inject enthusiasm into her voice even as a chill ran through her veins. "That's great, isn't it? It's what you wanted."

"Yeah." He frowned.

"Why the long face then?" She glanced about and saw Rue watching them. "What's happened?"

"It comes with conditions."

"What do you mean, conditions?" She didn't like the sound of this. The whole thing had given her a bad feeling right from the start.

"It's a dangerous place."

"Where exactly?"

"At present, El Salvador is our aim."

"El Salvador." Megan had heard of it, but she knew nothing about the country. "Okay."

"And the studio can't offer us any protection."

"What does that mean?"

"Their insurance just won't stretch that far."

"But you need protection, right? If you're going to be interviewing farmers who are working for drug dealers. What if the dealers, the gangs, show up? They're not going to be happy." She paused, pushing images of scary men with guns from her mind. "You'll need protection, James."

"Yes, we will. But I don't want you to worry." He reached for her hand. "Because Grant and I will get it covered. I have some contacts. Some guys we can pay to keep a watch over us."

"Grant and you. What about the rest of the team?" It couldn't just be James and his cameraman going, surely. That was ridiculous. Safety in numbers made sense.

"It's me and Grant, just us. It's the way it's always been, Megan."

"But I thought…"

"That we worked in big teams like down on the beach." He shook his head. "No, investigative journalism on the frontline doesn't work like that."

"You make it sound like a warzone." Suddenly her skin didn't feel so warm anymore. In fact she was goosebumped. James couldn't go to a warzone. That didn't make sense. Not now. Not now they had each other. What if something happened to him?

"It's a frontline on the war on drugs," he said, squeezing her hand. "The jungle farms are where they're manufactured, it's where the journey starts. The drugs go on to be distributed and do immeasurable harm, but they've also left a trail of destruction and terror in their wake."

"And if we know this already, why do you need to go?"

"I've told you before. This needs exposing. Drug cartels control the farmers and their land with violence and corruption, and the world is blind to it. The farmers' story needs to be out there for all to see. It needs exposing, maybe then the US government will take action."

"By you?" Of course she knew the answer to that. "Exposing by you."

He nodded.

She pulled her hand away from his and pinched the bridge of her nose. The alcohol and bubbles in the champagne had given her a pleasant buzz, but now it was like tinnitus ringing in her ears. It had been on the cards, this assignment, this next project. But she now realised she'd been burying her head in the sand, hoping it wouldn't ever come to fruition.

She'd liked it when James was making a safe documentary about lifeguards down on Santa Monica Beach. She'd known where he'd been and what he'd been doing. It was safe, too. But a trip to dangerous Central America with only Grant for company and a few paid heavies? That was scary stuff and she didn't want it to happen.

"It's my job," he said, waving away a waiter with a tray of food. "You knew this about me when we met. That I make documentaries that are on the edge. I don't do the fluffy stuff."

"Fluffy stuff?"

"Yes, you know, fashion, gossip, shoes."

"You think my work is fluffy?" She stared at him, her eyes wide.

He frowned. "No, that's not what I meant."

"So what did you mean?" She wanted to rub out what he'd just said, because she knew full well what he'd meant.

His work was important and hers wasn't.

"Baby." He rested his hand on her arm.

She tensed.

"Don't be like that." He frowned. "You know I admire you greatly."

She pressed her lips together. How had everything gone from being so right to so wrong so quickly?

"You're an incredible business woman, you clearly have a talent for design and a flair for fashion."

"And fluff."

"No." He shook his head, the creases in his brow deepening. "That was the wrong word."

"Oh, should it have been frivolous, trivial, shallow, inconsequential?"

"No, none of that. Don't be like this."

Megan set her glass down and stood. Her limbs were twitchy, her back ached suddenly and she had a bitter taste in her mouth.

She moved past a group of people chatting, then, making sure she gave Rue a wide berth, headed to the very front of the boat.

Here it was silent as the bow cut through the water. She held on to the chrome rail and stared at the watery horizon.

She'd thought they were equal, her and James, and that finally she'd found someone who respected her and what she did. Yet it was clear he considered his work substantially more important than hers.

But worse than that, he was prepared to risk himself.

What would she do without him? It would be awful when he was there, in El Salvador, but what if…?

No. She couldn't even think about that. It was too terrible an outcome to contemplate. Besides, he'd made dangerous documentaries before and lived to tell the tale. He was obviously doing something right.

She dragged in a deep breath, hoping that a sob wouldn't rush into her throat.

"Megan."

He was behind her.

She tightened her grip on the rail as the wind buffeted her dress against her legs.

"Please don't be mad," he said, his words catching in the breeze.

"I'm not mad."

"So let's talk about this?" He put his hands on the rail, either side of hers, and his chest warmed her back. Their bodies moved together slightly with the gentle rise and fall of the boat.

"There is nothing to talk about."

"Of course there is."

"No. You're going. You've made your mind up."

"This was in the pipeline before we even met."

"No." She shook her head. "It wasn't. It was the seed of an idea, that was all, that's what you said. You hadn't submitted the proposal and even then, if I remember correctly, you expected it to get turned down like nine out of ten of proposals do."

"But it hasn't been turned down. They want me to do it."

"You could have done something else for your next documentary. Something closer to home, not as dangerous. This wasn't set in stone."

He was quiet.

She knew his silence was because she was right. He'd had a choice. He still did.

He touched his chin to her temple. "I'm sorry."

"For what?"

"For upsetting you."

Now those damn little tears pricked her eyes. It had been easier to be angry than admit she was upset. She sniffed and blinked rapidly. "I'm not upset."

"And I'm sorry for saying the word fluff. It's not what I meant." As he'd spoken, his lips had moved against her hair.

"I know what you meant."

"I don't think you do."

She sensed a note of irritation in his voice. Well it was tough, she was irritated, too. Irritated to hell and back that he thought he could risk his life, risk everything, to expose a cause that was best left to the military and politicians. It was their job, not his. He wasn't some one-man band whose mission was to save the world.

"It will all be okay," he said, resting his hands over hers. "I promise."

She turned to face him.

The sun was directly behind him, creating a fuzzy white halo around his head.

He'd slipped his shades on. Her reflection stared back at her in the slightly amber-hued lenses. Her hair was flicking out behind her and her eyes were wide. "You can't promise that, James. You can't promise that it will be okay."

His lips squeezed into a tight line.

"I know what we have is new," she said, "it's been a whirlwind and I never thought I'd end up here, in LA, with you. But I am and…and I don't want that to change."

"It won't. But I have to work. I have to pay the bills."

"You've won awards, for heaven's sake. There are other jobs in the industry that you could do to pay the bills. Jobs that won't put you in the firing line."

"I've been in the firing line before."

"And that scares the living daylights out of me."

He smoothed his hand over her hair. "Megan. Don't ask me not to do what I do best."

"I'm not."

"It seems to me that you are."

"No." She shook her head. "I'm asking you to think about me. I just want to be part of your decision making process, a factor in your reasons to go or stay." She reached up and took off his shades. She needed to see his eyes.

As she did so, the boat slowed.

She stared up at him, at the face that filled her dreams and her hopes for the future.

If he's around for that future.

The engine died and the sound of the music had a chance to spread, filling Megan's ears with a happy tune that didn't match her mood. She was aware of her dress and hair falling still.

"That's all I want," she said. "Is for you to think of me. If something happens to you, I...I'd be devastated"

He cupped her cheeks, pain crossing his face.

She knew he was struggling with this. That he wanted her to say, go, do your stuff, but she couldn't. The words just weren't there. "Please," she said. "Just think about it. Don't say yes just yet."

He nodded. Once. "Okay. I'll think about it."

4

James

"I'll be back about five." Megan pressed a kiss to James' cheek. "Will you be in?"

"Yes. I'm heading to the gym and then catching up with Grant."

He noticed she bristled slightly. It was the mention of Grant. Not that there was anything wrong with Grant, nor did Megan have a problem with him. She just knew that El Salvador would be the main topic of their conversation.

And for the last few days, El Salvador had been the elephant in the room. The one topic that had been kept under wraps, swept beneath the carpet, hidden like a crazy relative.

She flicked open her bag and pulled out a bottle of perfume. She sprayed her neck and wrists then dropped it back into her purse. "See you then."

And just like that she was gone, leaving behind a cloud of sweetly scented air.

He touched his cheek, the feel of her lips lingering there.

Was he crazy to risk what they had? This new relationship with Megan was as delicate as glass. She was a runner, he knew that. When the going got tough, she had a habit of kicking up her glittery heels and taking off. Except she was still here now. She'd promised she wouldn't run anymore, that when they had mountains to climb, she'd stay and work it through. Talk about it. Go hand in hand through tough times.

The same way he'd promised he'd think about turning down the chance to go to El Salvador and film his new documentary.

Not that it was a damn vacation he was planning. It would be full-on sweat, dirt and grime. No five star hotels for him and Grant. There'd be tents beside mosquito-infested swamps and trips through areas that no sane man should venture into. And the thought of negotiating with drug barons if caught on their land sent a shiver up his spine.

But the people there—the ordinary families who were being ignored and left to fend for themselves—that was something he couldn't ignore. His moral compass just wouldn't let him. People had rights, no matter how poor they were. The right to earn a living without living in fear. The right to choose how they earned the money in their pockets. And as for the damn produce, the cocaine and heroin, that was the devil's work and if he could make one jot of difference in getting it off the streets, he would.

Sighing, he stood and picked up his breakfast plate, which was littered with toast crumbs and a banana peel.

Megan was going to LA Hype with Brendon to organise an outfit. She was excited about appearing on *The Paul Piper Show* the following evening. Mainly, she said, to put the world straight regarding her and Tate Simmons.

James huffed at the thought of the blond heart-throb who didn't have two brain cells to rub together.

What a prat. As if he'd ever stood a chance with a woman like Megan. One thing was for sure, James would be glad when their names were no longer linked and he was doubly glad that was all it had been—one date that hadn't even ended in them leaving the venue together.

After clearing up his plate, he wandered into the bedroom. He pulled on a grey Nike T-shirt and slipped his feet into Asics sneakers. Perhaps Grant would join him at the gym before they grabbed lunch. He could do with a buddy while he worked out.

He reached for his phone and fired off a text.

Gym in 20?

A response came through within a few seconds.

See you there.

James smiled. It would do him good to hash through the current situation with Grant. Not that he'd get impartial advice—Grant was an adrenaline junkie, a risk taker, and he had El Salvador in his sights. Likely he'd say that Megan would have to suck it up and cope with the fact that they were going.

But at least he'd have someone to tell him why the hell he was going.

He pulled the bedroom doors shut. Megan liked them open as she got ready in the mornings. She said the sea air invigorated her for the day and made her feel wide awake.

As he flicked the lock, James thought about how special it was to have her in his life and his home. Her easy smile made him want to smile, her laughter made him crave more of it, and holding her in his arms, when he fell asleep and when he woke, made his life complete.

He grabbed his kit bag and headed out to the car. It was so different with Megan from how it had been with Jenny, his first wife. Jenny had been much more serious, focused, regardless of what she was doing, whether it was her work or making supper. That had appealed to him, for a long time, but now he realised that being with someone who had the fun gene appealed to him a lot more. He liked the fact that Megan could let her hair down and dance in a living room to crazy music, that she was as comfortable on TV and around celebrities as she was with her wacky friends. She was loyal, hard-working, serious about her business but also light-hearted and cool. She'd got the balance right. Not an easy thing to do and something he was still working on.

But with Megan at his side, he was getting there. She was showing him the way, making him be the best person he could be. He needed to lighten up a bit and she helped him do that.

The traffic was heavy as he joined the freeway and he hoped Grant wouldn't make too much of a start on his workout. He flicked on the radio and an advert blasted out for *The Paul Piper Show.*

"Don't miss exclusive interviews, tonight, on the Paul Piper Show. Paul is joined on the couch by directing legend Levison Albright talking about his new World War Two movie, which is up for an Oscar. Penny Jo, star of sitcom House Rules is also chatting, and the woman Hollywood has been biting at the bit to get to know, Megan Winter, the London shoe designer who has... allegedly...bagged Hollywood's hottest property, Tate Simmons, will also be with Paul. Hang about because there's also music from Rock Chix, who are storming the charts right now. HBN, ten p.m., be there or be square."

James huffed. *Tate Simmons, Hollywood's hottest property.* Shame the masses thought a prick who considered it perfectly acceptable to slap a women's arse in public was the subject of such adoration.

An opening appeared in the traffic and he put his foot down, the thrust of his BMW pushing him backwards in the seat. He gripped the steering wheel and weaved around several cars, an SUV and a bus. The wind in his hair, the speed, the powerful engine at his command, gave him a buzz, a shot of adrenaline.

And James had to admit, as much as he thought Grant was an adrenaline junkie, he was, too.

He pulled up at *Ziggy's Top2Toe Gym* and waited while the roof on his convertible slotted into place. He noticed Grant's motorbike parked in the shade.

Within a few minutes, James was heading into the training area. He always started off on the treadmill and luckily Grant did, too.

"Hey, mate." He slotted his water bottle into the holder and flicked the machine on.

"I'm already a mile ahead." Grant wiped his brow with

the sweatband on his wrist. "What kept you?"

"Traffic."

"Won't be any of that to worry about in the jungle." Grant grinned.

"Mmm." James started off at a walk, but as the speed increased he broke into a jog.

"What do you mean, mmm?"

James didn't answer.

"What's up?" Grant frowned.

"Megan. She's worried about me going."

Grant laughed. "Of course she is—she's got her head screwed on, that one, and you're going to a place where taking a bullet is a very real possibility. As is getting kidnapped, tortured and held to ransom by mad drug lords who think we're their ticket to an extra million dollars."

"Not helping, mate."

Grant shrugged and upped his speed slightly. "Just saying it how it is."

"It's causing me a major headache, though." Ahead of him was a row of screens. One was playing MTV, another CNN and the final one some show where members of the public were hashing out their relationship problems in a particularly uncivilised way. He was glad the sound was off and he had no intention of putting his headphones in.

"Headache?" Grant repeated.

"Yeah." He paused. "Megan really doesn't want me to go."

"Neither does my mother, but I'm going anyway."

James hadn't even thought about his mother's reaction, or his sisters' for that matter. He'd been so wrapped up in the woman his life seemed to orbit around that it hadn't entered his brain. "I can't imagine my family will be thrilled, but I follow a tell-them-what-they-need-to-know rule these days."

"Good plan. What they don't know, they don't worry about."

"Exactly, and seeing as my mother and one sister are in

England, they're not likely to find out."

"But you've got your sister and Roxy here in LA?"

"Yes, don't get together with them that often though." A pang of guilt tugged at his chest. He really should up his game when it came to spending time with his sister's family, who only lived a short distance away. He'd had Roxy come and visit in London for a while, but still, a bit more effort was required.

"Not so easy to pull the wool over Megan's eyes though, eh?" Grant said. "Not if she's living with you."

"That's the trouble."

"What, you wish she wasn't living with you?" Grant threw him a sideways look. "I thought you were as happy as Larry—you've been like the cat who's got the cream ever since you worked it out with her."

"Of course her living at my place isn't a problem. I'm in love with the woman, so having her in Malibu with me is perfect. The house feels like a home with her there, she somehow brings it to life. Stops it just being bricks and mortar and a few fancy pieces of designer furniture."

"Very expensive bricks and mortar. That's prime real estate you have there."

"True." It had cost James a packet but it was worth every penny. He loved his beachside home.

"But how long will she stay?" Grant asked.

"What do you mean?" James could feel his heart rate increasing as his muscles took up the rhythm of his run and he settled into it.

"I mean she's a UK citizen. She's here on a visa, that's not a limitless time frame to have your house alive, buddy. You're going to have to think about that sometime soon."

James stared at the screen playing MTV. Several women in skimpy clothes were doing a strange jerky dance in a grimy alley. "I know. That's something else I've got to get my head around and find a solution to."

"You do indeed." Grant took a slug from his water bottle.

James suddenly knew exactly what the solution was to

that particular problem. And the knowledge speared into his brain like an arrow with a message wrapped around it. The thought bloomed, blossomed, overruled. He'd been consumed with the dilemma of going to El Salvador but now something else took precedence.

"I'm going to ask her to marry me," he said. "Then she can stay. She'll be married to a US citizen, me."

Grant was staring at him as he pounded on his treadmill. He had a sheen of sweat on his brow and upper lip and his mouth was parted. He was silent for a moment then, "Are you ready for marriage…again?"

James shrugged. The thought of being with Megan, today, tomorrow, forever made him happy, so, from that, he deduced that he was ready for marriage again…to her. "Yes." He pulled in a deep breath, right to the base of his lungs, then blew it out. "I am."

"Well, congratulations." Grant shook his head. "Never thought I'd see the day."

"What, that someone might want to marry me? I'm not that bad."

"Well if you look past the surly, brooding persona and the fact that you're single-minded and determined to the point of obsession once you've got a bee in your bonnet about some injustice, then sure, you'll be easy to be married to."

"You're an idiot sometimes, you know that?"

"Just pointing out the facts."

For a few minutes they ran in silence. James had always known he wasn't easy to live with—that was one of the reasons his first marriage had hit the rocks. But it felt different with Megan, like she was the yin to his yang. Opposites attracted and all that.

But he should try harder—he couldn't deny Grant was right about that. Which of course meant doing what Megan had asked and reconsidering the decision to go to El Salvador. He needed to at least hash it out in his head and contemplate withdrawing the proposal.

"So, on a scale of one to ten, how much do you think we

need to make this documentary?" he asked Grant.

"Ten." Grant stared straight ahead.

"Oh, okay."

"Are you wimping out on me now you're going to be a married man?" Grant turned up the speed and pumped his legs and arms faster.

James knew the question had annoyed his partner. "No, not at all." He did the same, whacking up the speed a few more notches. It was good to run, even though he wasn't getting anywhere—it was using up nervous energy and somehow helping him to manage his thoughts, stretching them out so he could see them clearly.

"The thing is," Grant said, breathless now. "This is what you do, buddy. You're an investigative reporter, you make shit-hot, show-it-how-it-is pieces without glitter and fluff to make reality palatable to the masses. And you know what, you're damn good at it. We're damn good at it."

James was quiet. Fluff. Yeah, he'd messed up with that word, big time.

"And," Grant went on, "the way I look at it, if you hadn't gone and got hit in the heart by Cupid, the little menace, then we wouldn't be having this conversation, we'd be planning what we were taking, where exactly we were going and what shots were our priorities."

"Yeah…I know." James continued to sprint. He was going faster than Grant now. As if running away from the problem—the tear that was ripping through the fabric of his relationship with Megan.

"We've got to go," Grant said. "There's no two ways about it."

"But what if I don't?"

"I'll find another guy to work with, one who isn't shy of danger."

"I'm not shy of danger." Feeling like he'd peaked, he slowed his machine, glad to be returning to a jog. "Danger, I thrive on."

"Tell me about it. I've been there, at your side, camera

rolling in just about every damn scrape you've gotten into."

James couldn't deny that.

"My take on it," Grant said, "is this is a landmark case between you and your new lady."

"What do you mean?"

"If you give in now, this first time, and don't go, then that's it, she'll always have the final say in everything you do."

"No, she won't." James tutted.

"That's what they all say, buddy." He shrugged and slowed to a walk, reaching for his water bottle as he did so.

"This is different. It's putting our lives on the line."

"It's just as dangerous to allow someone else to rule your life."

"You know what, Grant?"

"What?"

"No wonder you're single." James could feel his temper rising.

"I might be single but I'm not celibate."

"Yeah, well, one-night stands never did do it for me."

"They did that one time back in—"

"Shut it. We said we'd never mention Tokyo again."

Grant chuckled. "All I'm saying is fall in love, sure, but don't get squashed under her thumb. You've spent too long building up this career, getting to the top of your game, to let a pretty face and a sexy body tumble it all down."

"Megan is more than that."

"Of course she is, otherwise you wouldn't be thinking about marrying her."

"Well, proposing at least." He turned off his running machine then came to a halt.

"She'll say yes." Grant slotted his towel behind his neck and also stopped his treadmill.

"You think?" James hoped she would, but there was no guarantee, especially when he told her he'd reconsidered going to El Salvador and still had every intention of going.

5

Megan

"You still watching this?" Megan asked, smiling as she passed Brendon a glass of iced water.

"It's just so…you made me so…very proud." He pressed one hand over his chest and took the drink, fluttering his eyelashes as he did so. "Who would have thought it, my little sweetpea, holding her own with Paul Piper."

"Well, I just answered his questions." She sat next to Brendon and put her feet up on the soft leather stool James kept by his sofa. She was tired and her eyelids were heavy.

"Oh no, they weren't questions. He'd tied you up to a stretching rack and was turning that handle, pulling your limbs from their sockets, trying to make you tell all. He was going for the jugular, wanting to trip you up, reveal that there had been some rumpy pumpy between you and Tate." He pointed the remote at the TV. "This bit, watch."

"I do know. I was there." She laughed. Brendon had been like a mother hen clucking around her before she'd gone on the chat show—fussing with her dress and straightening the perfectly neat diamante shoulder straps over and over again. He'd fretted with her hair and makeup and polished her Silverdust shoes to the point she'd had to ask him to stop—it had been that or kick him in the shins.

"So, Ms Winter…" Paul leaned over his desk, fingers knotted and a salacious grin in place. "Do tell all. Spill the beans, what is Tate Simmons *really* like off camera?"

"He's polite and charming and fun to be around." Not entirely true, but Megan had smiled through the words anyway.

"And is that how he stole your heart?"

The other guests were studying her intently. Megan hadn't noticed that at the time. But the old director and young actress were hanging on her every word.

"Did he dazzle you, seduce you, make you feel like you were in heaven?" Paul licked his lips and raised his eyebrows.

Megan laughed softly. "There was no seducing. He needed a date to the awards and I went with him. That's all there is to it."

"And afterward?" Paul winked at the camera, a weird, over-exaggerated gesture. "Surely he's irresistible to all women? What with that body and that smile."

"Afterwards I went home. Alone." Also not true, but she was hardly going to say that she'd met up with James Carter, award-winning director of Poor Choices, on the beach and tumbled into bed with him. Not on national TV anyway. "Tate and I are just friends. I wish him well in all that he does."

"Oh, and does that include narrating the new series about the buff, sexy lifeguards down at St Monica Beach?"

Megan stared at the TV and was aware of Brendon fidgeting next to her. She recalled the feeling of dread, at this moment, when she'd been on the show. As the screen behind Paul flickered to life, she'd known full well what had been about to be played. And she'd been right, it was a spectator's iPhone video of Tate and James brawling on the beach. Well, brawl was perhaps a step too far, but certainly a few punches had been thrown and she'd been strutting straight towards the camera, a look of horror on her face.

"Tate Simmons certainly seems keen on you. Keen enough to bring out his Neanderthal side and take down another admirer," Paul said with a chuckle. "Not just another admirer, but none other than award-winning director James Carter."

"That was below the belt," Brendon said, banging down his water and folding his arms with a huff. "What kind of professional shows footage like that? It's a fuzzy phone video, not even in focus."

"A chat show host who makes a living from gossip," Megan said. "But at least I put the record straight. Now the world knows Tate and I are not an item. It's not pubic knowledge that James and I are together either, but still, at least my name is no longer linked to Tate's."

"And not before time."

Megan turned at the sound of James' voice. "Hi, you're home. Did you have a nice lunch?"

"Yes. Though, of course, as soon as I said I was dating Megan Winter, my sister was desperate to hear all about you, and now, naturally, wants to meet you."

Megan smiled. "I'm looking forward to meeting her, too. Next time I'll make sure I can join you when you go over to see her."

"She'd like that." He leaned across the back of the sofa and pressed a kiss to her cheek. "Why are you watching this again?"

"Brendon put it on."

"Yes, I like how your lady puts Paul Piper in his place," Brendon said, turning the TV off then dropping the remote on the soft cushion. "Not many people can."

"She certainly did that."

Megan finished her water and stood. "Are you staying for dinner, Brendon?"

"Oh, no, no." He hopped up. "I have a hot date with Zane—we're hitting Downtown and going to this cheeky little rumba bar. Apparently they have dancing waiters that wear tiny mardi gras outfits that leave nothing to the imagination."

"Sounds fun."

"It will be." He gave Megan a quick peck on the cheek. "Catch you tomorrow, and be warned—Paul Piper was just a warm up for Lavinia Heat. That woman will be like going under a grill on that stretching rack."

"It will be fine, I'm a guest there to talk about shoes, not my private life." Megan laughed. "Oh, and did that new delivery of shoes come in? Enid said they should be here by now."

"Yes, they did. Zane texted me earlier." He frowned. "We're going to have to expand into more shops soon. I've got that on my to-do list and it's top priority tomorrow."

"I agree." She watched as he scooped up a bright yellow cardigan that had vibrant limes embroidered all over it.

"Bye, sweetpea," he called, giving a backwards wave as he headed out of the door. "See you, Hot Guy."

Megan turned to James.

He wasn't there.

The study door was open so she wandered in. "What else have you got planned for today?" She rested her hands on his shoulders and hovered her nose over his hair, enjoying the scent of his shampoo.

"Just a few emails and then perhaps a walk on the beach with the woman of my dreams." He was tapping away, working through his inbox.

"That sounds like a plan." She didn't mean to look but she noticed an email he was writing to Rue that Grant was copied in on. The words filming starts in three weeks jumped out at her.

"What filming starts in three weeks?" The words slid off her tongue as her heart rate ramped up. Her knees suddenly felt weak.

He stopped typing then spun in his chair to face her.

She looked down at him. "You're going, aren't you?" She paused. "You've made up your mind."

He sucked in deep breath and stood.

She stepped back until her shoulders hit the wall and knocked against the picture of the rainforest. It couldn't be true. He knew how she felt about El Salvador.

"Megan." He frowned. "You have to understand it from my point of view."

"I've tried, really I have, but I just can't understand why you'd willingly put yourself in so much danger. This isn't your war."

"But it has to be someone's."

"Leave it to some other do-gooder then."

"Do-gooder, is that how you see me?" He raised his eyebrows.

"To a certain degree, yes. The same way I'm fluffy."

"I never said you were fluffy." He stepped closer.

She tore her gaze from his face and stared at the top two buttons on his neat black shirt. They were undone and his tanned chest was just visible.

"Megan." He stroked her cheek with the back of his finger. "This is who I am. I have thought about not going, I really have. Discussed it with Grant and laid in bed at night thinking about it. You asked me to take your feelings into consideration and I have, a lot."

"But it didn't make any difference."

"It did, a massive difference. If it hadn't been for you I wouldn't have hesitated—hell, I'd probably be there now. Just packed up and gone. But I've pondered on it, thought about the risks and consequences to my actions a hell of a lot more than I otherwise would have." His voice quietened. "Having you in my life has made me wake up and see what I could lose."

"Other than your life."

"I hope it doesn't come to that."

"Me, too." She looked up at him. His eyes were narrowed and little creases had formed at the sides. He appeared tired, evidence he'd endured the sleepless nights he'd mentioned.

She hated that she'd caused him angst by being so worried, but it had been necessary. He had to wake up and smell the roses, see what he was doing. Heck, he had family, too—what about them? "What did your sister say when you told her?"

He glanced away and dropped his hand to his side.

"You didn't mention it, did you?"

"No." He shrugged. "I don't usually bore her with the details of my work, so why start now?"

"Because you know she'd be as worried as I am."

"And I hate that, don't you see?" He held out his palms. "I hate that you're so worried—it's me at risk, not you."

"But…but you're what I care about."

"So don't try and stop me being who I am, Megan, it's suffocating. I make documentaries that sometimes require me to push boundaries, take risks. I can't stop doing that and get a job in Walmart just so you don't worry about me."

"Don't be ridiculous. I'm not asking you to get a job in Walmart, I'm just asking you to stay out of warzones. You're not military trained, nor are you a politician with diplomatic protection." She paused. "And I'm sorry if caring about you is suffocating. I never meant to be such a choking influence in your life."

Her eyes stung, her chest was tight. She marched past him, needing air and feeling suffocated herself. To think that in a few weeks' time he'd be dodging landmines and bullets and men out to kill him. She wanted to be sick. Nausea flooded her stomach and she swallowed rapidly as she headed to the decked balcony.

The smell of the ocean greeted her and she pulled in great lungfuls of air. Glancing about, she saw the beach was deserted. Just the way she needed it.

Opening the gate that led to their private steps, she then headed downwards, the sun's heat spreading on her shoulders.

She glanced back. He wasn't following. She was glad. She wanted to be alone. To digest what he'd told her. No, what she'd seen, because he hadn't actually told her, she'd spotted it in an email. When had he been going to break the news? When it was all set up? The day before he left?

Her bare feet sank into the warm sand as she made for the shoreline. Today the waves were small crests that sloshed in and ebbed away in a steady fizzing rhythm.

She headed north, not wanting the sun in her eyes and, with her arms wrapped around herself, set off at a dawdling pace. London right now was cold and grey—she'd been glad to be away from that. The sunshine in LA was a treat. But inside, at her core, it made no difference. She was *cold and grey*, and when James went away, she'd be freezing and without colour. How on earth was she supposed to cope? She'd be distracted on Lavinia's show. She'd be alone at Georgie's wedding.

She stopped. Pressed her hands to her face. Shit. She'd be alone at Georgie and Tom's wedding. James wouldn't be there. Not if he was chasing some drug cartel story around Central America. *How am I going to explain this to Georgie and Brendon?* And what was more, she'd been so excited about showing off her handsome new man to all her friends back in London. James was quite the catch. Not only that, they were in love, which had to be the ultimate goal. It had gone horribly wrong for her with Dylan but she'd picked herself up and was flying high.

A sob bubbled up from her chest and caught in her throat. More than anything she was scared—so damn scared of losing James.

If starting her own business had frightened her, or jilting Dylan at the altar had terrified her, they paled into insignificance with the actual reality of James being hurt in any way…or worse.

But she'd hurt him. Given him sleepless nights. Asked him to put his principles and his need to be a positive influence in the world to one side.

She'd been cruel and unreasonable.

"Baby, come here."

He wrapped his arms around her pulled her close.

"James," she whispered into his shirt. "I'm sorry."

"What for?" He rubbed her back.

"For asking you not to go."

"You asked because you cared." He kissed the top of her head, his lips lingering there. "I understand that."

She could hear the strain in his voice and feel the tension in his body.

A wave skittered around her bare feet, tickling her ankles.

She leaned more heavily against James, needing his strength and not wanting to imagine being without his touch for any length of time. "I do care, more than care, I love you, which is why I'd like to wrap you in cotton wool and keep you safe forever more." She looked up at him.

He raised his eyebrows. "Cotton wool?"

She pressed her palm over his cheek. His sprinkle of stubble scratched her skin. "You know what I mean."

"I do." He brushed a kiss over her lips.

"But…" She looked away.

"What?"

"I can't pretend I'm not upset that you won't be able to come to London with me, for Georgie's wedding."

"Oh, damn." He frowned. "Sorry."

She glanced down at the ground. The sand around their feet had indented, the waves sucking it away.

"But you'll have a nice time, with your friends."

"I wanted to be with you." She couldn't help the small whine in her voice. She'd already been thinking about how much everyone would love James. Not only that, but a few days in London, together, having fun. It appealed to her very much.

"There'll be other times. I promise." He smoothed his hands over her hair and studied her face. "You're tired."

"So are you."

He smiled. "Come on, let's go back and chill out. Forget about the rest of the world, for today at least."

"I like that plan."

He released her and steered her away from the waves slightly.

Megan hooked her fingers into the waistband of his jeans and pressed in close. There was nothing else for it—she'd just have to be brave. Put up and shut up. Thank goodness she'd have Brendon in LA with her when James was away. Without him, she'd go round the bend with worry.

As they walked in silence, she studied the small stones and pebbles that danced on the shoreline, crossing and rushing over each other in the rippling waves. She spotted a shell, a beautiful swirl of the palest pearlescent pink. Stooping, she picked it up. "This is pretty."

"It is." He stopped and pulled his hand from his pocket. "Let me see."

She passed it to him then pushed her hair from her face. The wind was picking up.

"There's something in it," he said, shaking the shell.

A tiny tapping sound came from within.

"A creature?" she asked, taking it back when he offered it.

"No, I don't think so." He grinned. "See what it is."

She tipped it into her palm. A gold ring tumbled out.

"What…?" Megan gasped. She reached for it and examined the large pale blue stone that was circled with diamonds. "James?" She looked up at him.

He was smiling, but there was a twitching tendon in his cheek.

"What is this?"

"It's an engagement ring." He took it from her, held it between his thumb and index finger, and dropped to one knee.

She clasped her hand over her mouth. *Is this really happening? Is this what I think it is?*

"Megan Winter, would you do me the honour of becoming my wife?" he said, ignoring a wave that skittered up and soaked his bent knee.

"But?" She pressed her hands over her cheeks. "I…"

His smile faltered. "I love you. I want you here, with me, not just in America but in my home, our home. Being my wife makes that possible."

She opened her mouth to speak. If this was just about her getting a green card…

"And before you say it, this isn't for visa reasons, it's because I want to spend the rest of my life with you."

Still she didn't say anything. Her head was spinning, her body felt like it was floating.

"And I want you to know how much I care for you," he

went on. "And that I will always consider your feelings, no matter what, from this point forward." He reached for her left hand and slipped the ring onto her finger. "And when I'm in El Salvador, knowing you're here, wearing this, waiting for me. That will be my first and last thought of each day and I will come back to you."

"James, I..."

He stood and cupped her cheeks. "Just say yes."

"Yes." A tear welled and overspilled, trickling down her cheek. "Yes. I will marry you."

"Thank God for that." He pressed his lips to hers and dragged her close.

She went up onto her tiptoes, draped her arms around his neck and became lost in the kiss. James wanted to marry her, spend his life with her.

She hadn't seen a marriage proposal coming, but she'd barely had to think about it to know that saying yes was the right thing to do. Being with him, in his arms, in his life, it felt so natural.

He deepened the kiss and spun, kicking up water as he did so. It splashed on her legs and she giggled against his mouth.

"I'll make you so happy, I promise," he said.

"You already do."

6

"Well cover me in tomato juice, stir me up and call me a Bloody Mary." Brendon grabbed hold of Megan's left wrist. "What the bejeepers is this rock the size of a small planet doing on your finger?"

Megan grinned. A bubble of sheer joy welled within her.

"Well?" Brendon demanded. "Tell all."

"It's what you think it is?" Megan's cheeks ached, she was smiling so much, and her heart was tripping along at a crazy rate. Everything was a little blurred, fuzzy—it was as if only she and James and the engagement existed.

Or at least that was what she was telling herself…for now.

"Hot Guy went and did it? He got down on one knee and popped the question." Brendon was hopping on the spot, the soles of his smart leather shoes tapping on the hallway floor of the house he rented in Venice Beach.

"He did, got a little soaked in the process."

"What?" He frowned. "Oh, never mind. Come here, you lucky, lucky mare." He snatched hold of her and pulled her into a tight hug. He then spun her around over and over.

Megan laughed and clung to him.

"Another wedding. You know I love weddings—you and Georgie keep me well-fuelled." He reached for her hands again and held them outwards. "And you do make such a beautiful bride."

"Well, I'm planning on this being the last time I wear a wedding dress."

"Oh, never say never."

"Brendon." She released his hands and swiped him on the shoulder. "James is the love of my life."

He shrugged, still grinning. "I'm just saying…"

"Well don't." She held her hand out, studying the ring

as it caught the light coming through from the kitchen. "I want to start and end each day with him, forever."

"And who can blame you? I bet he's a devil in the sack, isn't he?" Brendon winked.

"I'm not telling you anything."

"Spoilsport." He pouted.

"Come on, we have to tell Georgie the news. I want her to be part of this."

Brendon glanced at the clock on the wall. "It will be morning there, we'll catch her before she heads for the office. Quick."

They dashed into the small room used as a study and Brendon brought his laptop to life.

"What's that?" Megan asked, pointing to a pile of boxes in the corner.

"Oh, a shoe delivery from Enid."

"They didn't go straight to LA Hype?"

"No, these are samples to offer to other stores. We have to branch out, remember?" He rolled his eyes. "No, you probably don't with all of your excitement."

"Of course I do. Just didn't expect this batch to arrive so quickly."

"Well, they have, and you're going to be pleased with the selection."

"Let me look?" She lifted the lid off the top box. Inside was a stunning mocha-coloured gladiator sandal that had tiny brass coins hanging from the top strap. "Wow, this is perfect now. The coins were too big before."

"I thought you'd be pleased." He pushed at a chair. "But sit, we want to catch Georgie Porgie Pudding and Pie before she turns into a super-efficient business woman for the day."

The tinny sound of FaceTime calling echoed around the small room.

Megan sat and fiddled with her ring. It felt alien on her finger but also perfectly right. James had told her that it had belonged to his grandmother, and when she'd died, her eternity ring and wedding ring had gone to his sisters, but his grandfather had wanted James to have this one to give to the girl of his dreams. She'd still been alive when he'd married Jenny, so this was the first time anyone other than his grandmother had worn it.

Megan's eyes had brimmed with emotion when he'd told her that, and she'd noticed his had been a little misty, too. The fact that it was the right size for Megan proved to them both, all the more, that they were meant to be.

"Hey, you two, what's up?" Georgie appeared on screen. Her hair and makeup were neat and she wore a smart white blouse and navy fitted blazer. "I'm just heading out the door." She glanced at her rose gold watch. "Can't be late, got a meeting with my staff."

"Well, they'll just have to wait," Brendon said, bouncing on his seat.

"But—"

"You're the boss, don't fret," he said. "And besides, we have news, the best news, news that will blow you away big time."

Her eyes widened.

Megan held in a giggle.

"Show her," Brendon said. "Show her." He reached for Megan's left hand. "Prepare to be dazzled, Georgie."

He shoved Megan's hand up against the screen so that the ring took centre stage.

Georgie was quiet for a moment, then, "Bloody hell."

"Is that all you've got to say?" Brendon said, casting Megan's hand aside and thrusting his face to the screen.

"I mean…wow, is that what I think it is?" Georgie shifted to try to look round Brendon.

"Yes." Megan nodded. "James proposed yesterday evening, on the beach."

"On the beach," Brendon exclaimed, sitting back. "That guy does nothing wrong, does he?"

"That's so romantic," Georgie said, smiling broadly and clasping her hands beneath her chin. "So utterly perfect."

"I think so." Megan looked at the ring again. She couldn't help herself. It was like a magnet. "And this was his grandmother's ring. She was married for over fifty years to James' grandfather."

"Well, if that's not a good omen I don't know what is." Brendon nodded with a serious look on his face. "Full of good karma, that ring."

"I hope so."

"Megan, I'm so excited for you," Georgie said. "I wish I were there to give you a hug, pop open a bottle of champagne with you."

"Oh, oh, champers, yes, I'll get some." Brendon jumped up then dashed from the room.

Megan smiled. "You are here, kind of." She paused. "How is it going with your wedding preparations?"

"Oh, not too bad. Mum is getting her knickers in a twist about her outfit. Apparently her sister has bought the same dress and is refusing to take it back and get something else."

"Whoops."

"Well, they are twins and they go to the same shops. It stands to reason they'd like the same thing. Trouble is, Mum has carefully co-ordinated dad's tie and handkerchief to her outfit and she simply won't be swayed."

"She is the mother of the bride." Megan shrugged. "That must give her priority."

"That's what I thought, but I learnt long ago to stay out of their squabbles. I've got in the middle in the past and next thing is, they've worked it out, laughing and joking, but I'm still in the wrong for whatever I said."

"Mmm, true." Megan could remember a few instances like that over the years. "So what's the dress like?"

"It's blue and purple with a few cerise splashes on it, kind of reminds me of grapes getting crushed, you know, in Spain when they're making red wine with their feet."

"Lovely." Megan laughed.

"Here we go, fizz." Brendon swept into the room, glasses and a bottle of prosecco in hand. "You'll have to have a virtual one, Georgie, it's too early for booze in the UK, even for you."

Georgie laughed. "I'll have you know I have a very strict one p.m. rule."

"Yeah, yeah." Brendon laughed and released the cork.

It fell to the floor and rolled beneath the desk. Quickly he poured the fizzing liquid into two flutes. "Here you go." He lifted his.

Megan did the same.

"To the future Mrs James Carter." He clinked the rim of his glass against hers.

"Congrats," Georgie said, miming taking a drink.

Still beaming, Megan sipped the bubbly liquid. To think that soon she'd be Mrs James Carter. A wife. And not just any old wife, but the wife of a wonderful, kind man who was making a difference in the world.

Suddenly her heart sank.

El Salvador.

She set down her drink and pulled in a deep breath.

"What? What is it?" Georgie asked, leaning nearer to the screen. "Megan?"

"Oh, Georgie," she said, shaking her head and frowning. "I've got something to tell you."

"What?" Brendon held his hands up, sloshing drink onto his knuckles. "Dear Lord above, tell, tell."

Megan pressed her hand over her chest. "Your wedding, Georgie, James isn't going to be able to make it."

Georgie was silent. Her eyes narrowed as though confused. "What? Why not? I thought you'd got flights organised..."

"I've got mine, but he's had a different kind of proposal accepted."

"What do you mean?"

"He's going to make a documentary about drug cartels using poverty stricken farmers to grow their produce. He's going to be in the middle of filming when you get married."

"But he can take annual leave," Georgie said then bit her

bottom lip. "Surely."

"It doesn't work like that in his industry. He's heading off in a few weeks to El Salvador. I don't know exactly how long he'll be gone for but it will be about a month, I think."

"A month!" Brendon screeched. "He can't leave his new fiancée for a month! What the hell is he thinking?"

"He can, it's his job." Megan had known she'd have to defend James for his decision but that didn't make it any easier. Not when she still wanted him to change his mind about going. But that wasn't likely to happen. Determined and driven was the sort of person he was, which, of course, was one of the reasons she loved him. He did what he said he was going to do and didn't shy away from hard work or risk.

"A month," Georgie said, "which will mean there's no way he'll make my wedding, it's in five weeks' time."

"I know. I'm so sorry. He's so sorry." She frowned and tried to beat down a wave of anxiety. Her eyes prickled with tears and her throat felt tight. James not making the wedding was only a small part of her reason for not wanting him to go.

"Oh, Megan," Georgie said. "It's okay, really it is. There will be other times we can all get together. Perhaps Tom and I can come out to LA later in the year. Tom's dying to meet him, and he will be even more so now that you're engaged."

"I'd like that."

Brendon sat next to her and wrapped an arm around her shoulder. "And don't worry, I've got your back. Zane can't make the wedding either."

"Which is a damn shame," Georgie said. "But I understand. It's his father's sixtieth on the same day so there's no contest."

"Oh, I didn't know that," Megan said, reaching for Brendon's hand. "Sorry."

"Not your fault, honey, just how life goes. There'll be other times, like Georgie said, but what's important is we'll all be there. And while Georgie is all loved-up during the first dance, you and me, sweetpea, can be wallflowers together."

That made Megan feel a bit better. She'd stick with Brendon, the way she usually did—if he felt sad she'd buck him up and if a meltdown threatened to consume her he'd keep her glued together.

She squeezed his hand. "Thank goodness we all have each other, eh."

"Absolutely." He pressed closer to her, crushing her shoulder to his.

"We have each other, even across the miles," Georgie said. Once again she glanced at her watch. "I really have to go, though, or my staff will sack me. I was late in yesterday because I'd been to the florist and got carried away and lost track of time. They'd run a meeting without me."

"Sounds like you've got a great team," Brendon said.

She smiled. "Yeah, they are pretty awesome. When Tom and I are on honeymoon I'll be able to completely relax, they're very competent."

"Talking of honeymoon, did you get it booked up yet?" Megan asked.

"Yes." She grinned. "We did."

"And…where are you going?" Brendon swirled his hand in the air. "Spill the beans, dish the dirt."

"New York. We've always fancied it."

"Oh, how romantic." Megan sighed. "Just think, The Empire State Building, Statue of Liberty, horse and carriage rides in Central Park, dinner at the Plaza."

"I know, plus we're hoping to get a trip up to Niagara Falls, too." Georgie was beaming.

"It sounds amazing," Brendon said. "And perfect. You'll be ready for a rest after the big day."

"Tell me about it." She leant forwards and blew a kiss at the screen. "I'm off. Congrats again, Megan. I'm thrilled for you. Give my love to James."

"Bye now, boss lady, catch you soon," Brendon said.

"See you." Megan waved.

Brendon shut the laptop and spun to face her, his knees brushing hers. "Okay, Megan Winter, what else is going on?"

"What?"

"I can see you're ecstatic and that gem on your finger is where it should be, but…"

"But?" She glanced away. He knew her too well.

"You don't want him to go to El Salvador, do you?"

"No." Once again her eyes stung with the tears that rushed there. "I really don't."

"And why not?"

"Why not? Do you even have to ask?"

He took her hands and linked their fingers. "I get that it's dangerous, but he's a competent man."

"But he is still just a man, flesh and blood, he could get hurt. Bullets won't bounce off him."

"True, but think about it. He's been in some pretty dicey situations over the years, hasn't he?"

She nodded.

"And this is just another one."

"But I've got a bad feeling about it." She sniffed.

He released one of her hands and dragged a box of tissues across the desk, offering her one.

"Thanks." Megan dabbed at a tear running down her right cheek.

"Of course you've got a bad feeling about it. You haven't been around for any of the other stuff he's done."

"What do you mean?"

"You weren't on the scene. Didn't know him. But now that's different and him taking a risk affects you."

"I love him." Tears were rolling uncontrollably now. "Oh, Brendon, what will I do if something happens to him?"

"It won't."

"You don't know that."

He sighed and pressed his lips together, staring into her eyes. "You're right, I don't know that. But what I do know is that man of yours is used to living on the edge, he's sharp, got his wits about him, and now, on top of all of that, he has you to come home to. He's not going to do anything to risk his future with you, is he?"

Megan sniffed. Her cheeks were hot and her chest ached with the strain of holding in sobs. "I hope not." She thought back to their first proper date at Bettino's, a quaint Italian restaurant in London. Little had she known back then that James would become so important to her. She remembered him mentioning his next project, but had never imagined it coming to fruition would feel like the end of her world.

"So what you have to think about," Brendon said, holding up her left hand, "is that your fiancé needs you to be strong when he's gone. The last thing you want is him worrying about you and being distracted."

"I guess you're right."

"Of course I'm right." He tutted. "This is what it's all about, marriage, supporting each other. Still being individual people. Dylan tried to morph you into someone you weren't. The person he wanted you to be." He paused. "So don't you try and do that to Hot Guy."

"I won't. I'm not." She was horrified at the thought. "It's totally different." And if she was honest, she was a bit cross that Brendon had drawn a comparison.

He reached for his drink and took a big gulp. "Yes, it's totally different." He smiled suddenly. "So what did your parents say when you told them about your engagement to a hot TV exec?"

"My parents." She ran her fingers through her hair. "I haven't told them yet."

"You haven't told them." He opened the laptop with a flick of his wrist. "Seriously, girl, I need a raise. Not only do I manage your business half the time, the other half I manage your life. Without me, you'd be a stiletto without a heel, a sandal without a strap."

She giggled suddenly. "A mule without a wedge."

"Exactly."

Any tension between them evaporated the way the fizz did as it sparkled over the rim of their glasses.

"Right, time to tell Mummy and Daddy the good news," he said, straightening his T-shirt and checking his carefully styled hair. "They're going to be coming to another wedding."

"But..." She did a quick calculation of the time in Australia. "It's late over there."

"Ah, that's fine. How often do they find out their eldest daughter is getting married?"

"Well, this is the second time."

"Second time lucky."

7

Three weeks later

Megan stood on the deck looking out to sea. A slew of fat-bellied clouds hovered on the horizon and she wondered if a storm was coming their way. She hoped not. James would be flying soon and the last thing she wanted was for him to start his trip to El Salvador surrounded by thunder and lightning. She'd been praying for weeks that it would all go smoothly and he'd be home before she knew it.

She could hear him now, moving about the bedroom, finalising his packing. It had been a major operation getting organised. It seemed everything had to be specialist for jungle survival, from clothes to tents, emergency medical equipment and rations packs. And that was before the insect repellents and the filming apparatus, though to be fair, Grant took charge of most of that. Still, James would do his share of carrying the load.

Megan couldn't help but think he'd be like a packhorse going through the jungle if they ended up on foot. The temperature would be hot and humid and the terrain difficult. Walking didn't seem like their safest option.

She hoped they would stick to a vehicle.

Apparently they were being met in San Salvador by two ex-military guys, Special Forces, who were being paid to be James' and Grant's eyes and ears, or at least that was the expression James had used. She didn't need him to spell it out that they'd be carrying some serious weaponry to keep them all safe—she could only pray that two bodyguards would be enough if things got nasty. When she'd voiced her concern and suggested that perhaps four or even six fully loaded chaperones would be better, she'd been quickly told how much their services cost, which had buried that idea.

She swallowed. She had a strange taste in her mouth. It was fear, she was sure of it, but she was trying to ignore it. Now was her time, Brendon had reminded her again the day before, to be the supportive, understanding and encouraging fiancée James deserved. He didn't need to have guilt on his conscience because he was leaving her to go to work, nor did she want him worrying about her while he was gone. He had to keep his mind on the job, be focused, stay safe.

She popped a mint into her mouth then set the empty packet aside. She'd bought two packs the day before and eaten both. It seemed they were addictive. But they were just so refreshing she couldn't resist.

Glancing at her watch, she stepped through the open French doors into their bedroom. Having a balcony overlooking the beach would never get old. She loved it.

She also loved the man standing with his back to her now. He wore dark green cotton trousers and a black T-shirt that stretched across his shoulders, highlighting his muscles. He'd had his hair cut shorter than normal and she loved the way it felt when she ran her fingers through it.

He must have sensed her there because he turned, a compass in his hand. "Hey, baby. You okay?"

"Yes, are you?"

He nodded. "Final check."

"Are you sure you've got everything you need?"

"Yes." He slipped the compass into a side pocket of the large, camouflage-patterned rucksack he was taking. "And if I haven't, well, it's too late now."

"Passport?"

"Yes, that's here." He touched a different pocket.

"Bug spray?"

"Yes." He nodded and took a step towards her.

"Mosquito net?"

"Yep."

"Spare socks?"

"I have everything I need." He wrapped his arms around her waist. "Except for you."

"I don't think I'd fit in your bag." She clutched the material of his top, squeezing it tight as though doing so might keep him with her.

"Mmm, could be worth a try." He smiled as he stared down at her.

She swallowed. There was a tightness in her chest, but she'd promised herself she wouldn't cry, at least not until after he'd gone. Then she could break down all she wanted. She could sob into her pillow, scream her frustration, start counting the days until he came home.

"Are you sure you're okay?" he asked.

"I'm fine." She nodded. "Really I am."

"Are you still going out with Brendon and Zane for dinner this evening?"

"I don't know." She didn't feel like it, not now. She wanted to be alone. And besides, she wasn't hungry.

"You should. I don't like to think of you sitting on your own, worrying. It won't help."

"I won't be worrying this evening. You're just catching a flight then staying in a hotel, aren't you?"

"Yes, tonight we have a proper bed at least."

He didn't need to add that after that she could start worrying.

"So go out," he said, "have a few drinks, plan world domination of the shoe industry."

"I think Brendon is already doing that."

"And with the Lavinia Heat show tomorrow, I'm sure you'll be a step closer to doing just that."

"Being on national TV will certainly be a distraction." She paused. "You know Lavinia will be all over my ring and our relationship."

"So tell her everything." He grinned and ran his hands down her back. "Because I want the world to know that you're mine and I'm in love with you."

"Everything?" She raised her eyebrows.

"Well, maybe don't tell her what I'm about to do to you."

"Oh, and what's that, then?"

He kissed her and tugged at the zipper on her skirt. It loosened then pooled at her feet.

A tug of longing went through her. They'd made love the night before with breathless intensity, clinging to each other in a hot and sweaty tangle of limbs. They'd both known that joining had to keep them going for the coming weeks, but now it seemed James wanted more.

Not that she was complaining.

She kicked the skirt away and reached for the button on his trousers. After popping it open, she undid the fly and pushed them down, along with his boxers.

"Grant will be here soon," James said, kissing over her cheek and reaching for the base of the cropped top she wore.

"So be quick," she said, raising her hands so he could strip her off.

He nuzzled her neck and stepped out of his pants. "Not too quick."

"Well no, not that."

Her bra joined the rest of the clothes piling up on the floor, as did her knickers.

Still kissing her, James manoeuvred them to the bed.

The sheets were cool on Megan's back as she stretched out, but James' body was warm as he hovered over her.

"I love you so much," he said, shucking his T-shirt off. "The last thing I really want is to be away from you."

"Shh…" She stroked her hand over his hair. "It's okay, I understand."

"Thank you." He paused. "For saying that."

She cupped the back of his neck and pulled him lower so their mouths connected.

He slotted between her legs and pushed in. They fitted so perfectly together, they were so in tune, so right. James filled her senses and made her feel complete.

She closed her eyes, adjusting to him, and hooked her legs

over his.

Within minutes she was breathless and on the edge. The curtains fluttered on the breeze that tickled her hot skin. James picked up the speed and she clung to him, lost to the way he made her feel.

He groaned, sensing her pleasure, and matched her moment of release.

"Please…come back…safe…" she said, clutching his shoulders.

"I will." He went onto his elbows and pushed her hair from her face. "I have everything to live for, so of course I will."

"Remember you said you'd never upset me?"

He paused, then, "Yes."

"Remember that. Don't take risks. If there are two options, take the safest one. No gambling with your life…because it's my life, too." She slid her hand down his warm chest and cupped his left pectoral muscle. "My heart is yours."

"Five minutes to air time."

Megan stared into the mirror. The makeup girl had been heavy-handed. Megan's skin was thick with foundation and her eyes were so smoky they were nearly black. But it was too late to change that now. This was her, ready for her special guest appearance on *Lavinia Heats It Up.*

She stood, patting her hair, which had been twisted into an elaborate up-do then sprayed to within an inch of its life. The Californian sun had lightened it, and with her new tan she was starting to look like she belonged.

Pressing her hand to her stomach, she stood. She really shouldn't have eaten that doughnut—it wasn't sitting well now that nerves had taken hold. But it would be okay—that was the last thing Brendon had said before he'd gone to take his seat in the audience. All she had to do was smile, chat shoes and if Lavinia mentioned James, then that was fine, too.

"Come on, come on." A man with a clipboard appeared around the door again. "You're on."

"Yes, of course." Megan rushed to follow him.

Out in the corridor she was met by Lavinia.

"Hello, my little English poppet, how are you doing?"

"I'm good thanks, you?"

"Very well." She smiled, her lips, coated in sticky purple lipstick, stretching wide. "Even better, because a little birdy tells me you have news."

"News?"

"Oh, don't play dumb with me." She cackled as she walked away, motioning for Megan to follow. "I know that you and that stud you were on Rue's yacht with are engaged."

Megan smiled. "Yes, we are."

"And it's public knowledge?"

"Well, it's not a secret."

"Oh goody," she rubbed her hand together. "Does that mean I get the exclusive?"

"I don't see why not." Megan's heart beat a little faster. Soon the world would know that she would be marrying James Carter. But that was all they'd know. She wouldn't say a word about where he was and what he was doing right now. That was his business and he'd tell the world his story in his brilliant way when he got home.

When he gets home.

She twisted her hands together. It had barely been twenty-four hours since he'd left and it felt like there was a vacuum next to her, a space where he should be.

"Tell me, is he as hot in bed as he looks like he is?" Lavinia strutted through a door held open by a member of the floor crew then onto the set. "He's got that brooding darkness that always equates to some great between-the-sheets skills."

"A lady never tells," Megan said.

"Ah, that's what I love about you British, so reserved when it comes to sex."

"I guess we just like to keep our private lives private."

"Not an easy thing to do in this town, little one." She indicated a seat. "You're there. Just smile and nod and do your best not to curse. We say pretty much anything here but dropping the F word gives the producer hives."

"I don't plan on swearing."

"Good girl."

Megan sat still as a tiny microphone was attached to the collar of her blouse. She glanced about. Two huge cameras were set on wheels and, behind them, a sea of expectant faces were in the shadows, the live audience the show was renowned for. But the actual set had been created to look like a living room with a cosy fire, a bookcase and pictures. The TV on the wall was the centre of the show, with all the stars from A list to Z list having their images flashed up there and their outfits dissected.

"And five, four, three…" The director, a small man in tight red jeans and a black T-shirt, waggled his fingers.

"And hello and welcome to another edition of Lavinia Heats It Up." Lavinia crossed her long legs, flashing the lace top of her stockings.

The audience gave a ripple of applause.

"Tonight we have a treat," she said. "The one and only Megan Winter has joined us, and for anyone who has been living on a different planet, this is the lady who rocked up to the Sparkling Star Awards last month with none other than Tate Simmons."

A crescendo of ohhh made the hairs on the back of Megan's neck tingle and heat flushed over her chest. Why was she still being associated with Tate-bloody-Simmons?

"But." Lavinia held up her hands. "That's ancient history, isn't it, Megan?"

"Yes." Megan smiled at the camera. "It is."

"Come on, don't be shy." Lavinia waved her left hand in the air. "Show the world your bling."

Megan smiled and held out her hand, showing off her precious engagement ring to a camera that had zoomed in.

"And of course, the lucky man is none other than the gorgeous James Carter—not shabby on the award front himself, is he?"

"No, he's not." Megan nodded. "I'm very proud of him."

"And, just for the record." Lavinia leaned towards the camera. "I have seen these two lovebirds in action and let me tell you, they are the real deal and phew…what gorgeous babies they'll make." Again she cackled.

Babies?

Megan's cheeks were aching, her smile was so stiff. The heat was spreading around her ribs to her back. Being the centre of attention when it came to her private life was nowhere near as much fun as when it was all about her shoe designs.

"And talking of babies," Lavinia said, "we have had some of the cutest outfits this week on the babes of the rich and famous. Let's start with baby Heath, the daughter of Monty King and Rose Day. I mean, couldn't you just eat her up in that dress?"

A picture of an adorable toddler holding the hand of one of the stars of a popular crime drama flashed up on the screen. Megan had to agree, she did look adorable.

"Being dressed in Gucci at the age of two isn't for everyone, but Heath is rocking it."

Another picture flashed up, this time of twin girls, the daughters of a female action hero. They were in riding gear and, at aged eight, starting to work the camera with pouts and carefully placed crops.

Lavinia chatted for a moment or two about their top-end gear, then three more children were shown, all in super-expensive outfits that would probably only fit for a matter of months. Megan was pleased that all the comments were sugar coated—it seemed Lavinia kept her inner bitch under wraps when kids were involved.

"Now, Megan," Lavinia said. "You're one of the hottest names in shoe design right now, with red-carpet goers seeking your products and an exclusive new line in Rodeo

Drive. Tell us more."

"Yes, Winter Shoes is taking off, and it's great to see. I'd established myself in London, so now that LA is loving my heels and sandals, wedges and boots, I'm thrilled."

"I hear they're super comfortable to wear. My great buddy Amanda Rush has not stopped talking about hers. Combining glamour with something that doesn't give your face the appearance of a cat's ass is really special."

"That's good, that they're comfortable, that is. It's one of the things that I insisted on."

"And with a launch party, a little birdy told me, that had Greta Breen salivating to get a pair for the Oscars, you must feel like your dreams are coming true."

"The launch party was great fun and Greta is very charming."

"So what is it about shoes that's so special to a woman?" Lavinia leant forwards as though waiting to hear Megan divulge the meaning of life.

"It's the icing on the cake," Megan said, flashing a smile at the camera. "Whatever you're wearing, it can be made or broken with shoes. The wrong height, the wrong colour or fabric and it's derailed, but get it right and an outfit goes from fab to fabulous."

"I agree."

"And it's not just the aesthetics, it's how it makes a woman feel. A well-fitted pair of comfortable shoes is good for the soul."

"Ah, the soul, I get what you did there, Megan. Pun intended, I take it."

Megan held her own shoe out and laughed. "And I'm all about soles. My entire range have glittering soles, so they're pretty all over."

"Oh now that is adorable." Lavinia made a quick show of looking at the base of Megan's heels then turned to the screen. "Now let me tell you, glitter won't last long on Norma Hill's shoes. What on earth goes through your mind, Megan, when you see this kind of shoe disaster?"

A photo of a gorgeous blonde in a scarlet bikini flashed up. She wore high red heels and was clearly struggling to walk through deep, dry sand. Her body was thrown off kilter as she sank with each step, her arms at an awkward angle and a frown in place.

"Not the best choice for a day at the beach," Megan said.

"It's a no-brainer." Lavinia clapped. "What was the girl thinking?" She turned to Megan. "Seriously, is she out of her mind or what?"

"A nice pair of flats, sandals or flip-flops would be better."

"They would, but fashion-victim or what?" Lavinia cackled. "No wonder her last movie bombed—she clearly approaches acting the way she approaches a day at the beach, ill-prepared and full of nonsense."

Megan said nothing. The last thing she wanted to do was bad-mouth an actress live on air. Not a good start to a Hollywood career where she wanted the rich and famous, the stars and the elite, to be fighting over her shoes, not her words.

"And now to Tammy Rix, this is the opposite extreme, don't you think, Megan?"

Another picture flashed on the screen, this time of an actress Megan hadn't heard of. She wore a short summer dress that showed off killer legs and a rash of expensive-looking jewellery, but she'd combined it with tatty old moccasin boots, the sort Pocahontas would throw out because they were past their best.

"What a car crash," Lavinia said. "She must have had another one of her mental breakdowns that day." She turned to Megan. "Tell us what you think of this major disaster."

Megan pulled in a deep breath. She needed to say something positive yet at the same time not seem as if she thought it were a good look. "Well, personally, I'd have gone for a white strappy heel with that beautiful dress. Is it Valentino?"

"It is." Lavinia nodded. "Wow, an eye for dresses as well

as shoes."

Megan smiled. "I do like to keep watch on the big designers—it helps me see what's on trend and what's going to work the next season for my designs."

"Smart girl." Lavinia turned to the camera. "And on to news about..."

As she went into a long rambling spiel about a recent Hollywood wedding, Megan was glad of the respite. Lavinia certainly went at ninety miles an hour on her show.

Still, Megan believed she'd handled her guest slot well. She hadn't said anything that could be misconstrued or taken the wrong way.

She caught a glimpse of Brendon in the audience.

He was grinning and gave her the thumbs up.

The flutter of nerves in her belly slowed slightly.

Yes. She could do this. She could hold her own on American TV.

8

As the nine-fifteen Los Angeles to London flight took off, Megan gripped the armrests of her plush seat.

"You okay?" Brendon asked, flicking through Rainbows and Dreams magazine.

"Yes."

"Sure? You look a bit pale." He studied her closer.

"I'm fine, really. This bumpy ride is just making me feel a bit nervous."

"We've only just taken off." He frowned and finished the last of his gin and tonic, the lemon slice bumping his lip. "And so far, so good."

The ride wasn't turbulent—the weather was calm and they'd splashed out on first class seats which had been on sale. Megan knew it would be a comfortable overnight journey and hoped she'd get some sleep. The whirlwind of Lavinia's show then two more launch parties at various boutiques around the city had taken its toll. She was dog-tired after a crazy few weeks. Her bones seemed to ache with it and her eyelids felt constantly heavy.

She sighed and settled back in the chair. She wished James was with her. That had always been the plan. But of course he wasn't, he was in some jungle in El Salvador doing God only knew what.

She supressed a familiar wave of anxiety. Sometimes her worry for James consumed her and tears sprung to her eyes. Other times she buried it, like an ostrich shoving its head into the sand. It was just too scary to think about, too awful to contemplate. And the fact that she'd only heard from him once, when he'd landed in San Salvador, didn't help.

"There'll be no Wi-Fi," he'd told her, "and few landlines,

but if I can, I'll call. But if you don't hear from me for a few weeks, don't worry. It doesn't mean anything bad has happened, just that I'm out of communication."

How could she not worry? It seemed worry was her middle name right now. It had moved in, pulled up a chair and made itself comfortable.

"Shame we've had to cut our trip to London short," Brendon said, "there's a band playing at Torso I'd love to see."

"Anyone I know?"

"Barbarian. Heard of them?"

"No, sorry." She paused. "But you could stay and I'll head back on my own."

"As if I'd let you do that." He tutted and shoved his magazine into the pouch of the seat in front. "Besides, you need me."

"I do." She reached for his hand then gave it a squeeze. "You're the best PR manager a girl could ever wish for."

"I think we can safely say my duties extend well beyond PR." He rolled his eyes and grinned.

She smiled. "They do. I should give you raise."

"Well, I wouldn't say no to that, but maybe let's wait until we get you into Harrods first."

"That would be cool. There's something about that shop. Getting in there…you know?"

"Yes, you'll really feel like you've made it on the London scene."

"Exactly. And LA is going so well. Winter Shoes have definitely arrived there."

"As have you. Are you excited to be going on the Lavinia show again?"

"I think so. I'm still shocked that she's asked me to host a special edition when she's away. What an honour, and I've only been on once." She paused and took a sip of her sauvignon blanc. It tasted off so she pushed it away.

"Yes, but you were a natural, and she loves you." He giggled and put on a silly voice. "Her little English poppet."

"Much as she's a complete bitch to some of the stars, she's a softie really. I'm grateful to her. What with her and Zane in my corner, my shoes are becoming household names."

"Only people with households in Beverly Hills, Malibu and Bel-Air, sweetpea."

"Well, yes, true." She crossed her legs and sighed. "Where do you think Lavinia goes on holiday?"

"That's easy."

"Oh?" She turned to Brendon.

"To the clinic—she'll be having more fillers, Botox, a neck tuck. Then sitting recovering in some fancy spa in Indian Wells, the desert sun topping up her tan."

"And here was me thinking she'd be on a beach in Hawaii."

"And where would the fun in that be?"

Megan woke disorientated. She stared at the white ceiling with the pink lampshade she recognised then turned to the pink and silver striped velvet curtains that hung to the floor. Daylight peeked around them in golden shards.

Home.

Home in London.

James was her next thought. Where was he? Was he okay?

Her arms ached to hold him. Being in bed without him was cold and lonely. She knew the hollow feeling in her chest wouldn't go away until he was at her side again. Only then would she be able to breathe easily and truly relax.

She glanced at the clock. It was two p.m. on Friday. In exactly twenty-four hours, her best friend Georgie would be walking down the aisle. It was time to get up and get the show on the road.

Wearily she sat. As she did so, a wave of nausea bubbled up. It crested and consumed her. She rushed to the toilet—making it just in time. She hadn't expected to eat something dodgy on business class but it appeared she had. Maybe it had been the wine she'd sipped.

Afterwards she brushed her teeth and stared at her reflection in the mirror. The jetlag had really taken its toll. She had mauve bags under her eyes and, despite her living in the sun, the rest of her face was pale. Thank goodness she'd made time to get a trip to the hairdressers the week before. Having split ends really would break the camel's back right now.

She jumped through the shower, thinking that Marmite on toast might be just the thing. She fancied the saltiness, the stodge of bread. She was sure it would settle her stomach. Maybe it wasn't a bug—perhaps her innards were just complaining about being jetted around the globe.

Once dressed in jeans and a pale lilac vest top, and having managed tea and toast, she headed to Georgie's house. It was warm weather, the sun beating down on the London pavements, so she decided to walk, hoping the fresh air and the familiar scents of the city would revive her.

When she finally knocked on Georgie's black front door she was beyond excited to see the bride-to-be, and grinned in anticipation.

"You're here," Georgie squealed as she dragged Megan into a tight embrace. "At last. God, I've missed you so much. What took you so long? I need your help, oh, and you need to try on your dress. I've gone for a lemon torte for dessert, do you think that's okay? The caterers had a nightmare with their delivery of rum chocolate. But what if people don't like lemon? Brendon is here, just arrived and having a Bloody Mary."

Megan laughed and held Georgie at arm's-length. "Slow down, I can't keep up." She then dragged her into another hug. This was Georgie's special time. She and Tom were soul mates. They deserved their big day to go perfectly, then a lifetime of happiness and togetherness.

"I'll have you know a Bloody Mary is one of my five a day." Brendon appeared at the living room door holding a bright red drink. "Cheers."

"Are you sure about that?" Megan asked, grinning.

"Admittedly it's a stretch, but I've added celery to help my cause." He held up his drink. "Want one?"

"Oh, no thanks." She pulled a face. "I can think of nothing worse."

"Come on, first things first," Georgie said, yanking her farther into the house. "You need to try your dress on. It should fit fine, the seamstress at Covent Garden Brides does the bridesmaid dresses for royalty, you know. Couldn't be any more skilful or experienced."

"Wow, very fancy."

Georgie grinned and tugged at the zip on a crimson dress carrier. As she slid it down, she revealed shiny, coffee-coloured material.

"I love the colour," Megan said, clasping her hands beneath her chin. "When you said brown I wasn't sure, but..."

"It's lovely, isn't it?" Georgie carefully drew it out and held it up by the hanger. "It's because it's satin and such an exquisite cut, it really works."

"Let me try it on." Megan adored the dress and couldn't wait to wear it. She'd known Georgie was going for something off the shoulder and elegant, and this was really stunning and so sophisticated.

"Of course, what are you waiting for?" Georgie unhooked it and tossed the hanger onto the sofa.

Megan quickly stripped to bra and knickers—it wasn't the first time she had done so in front of her friends when trying things on.

"My cravat and cummerbund match." Brendon set down his drink. "We'll be the talk of the town."

"Stop talking and help me," Georgie said, fussing with the hemline.

Brendon rushed over and within a minute Megan was stepping into the dress.

The lining was cool and soft, the hem wrinkled slightly on the floor.

"Fine when you're in your pretty cream heels," Georgie

said, adjusting the ruches at the side that gathered to show off Megan's waist.

"Oh, it's divine." Brendon gasped.

"I love it." Megan looked in the full-length mirror Georgie had propped against the wall. "I'd never have gone for this colour."

"With your hair and tan it's amazing."

"I agree." Brendon stood behind her and slid the zipper up.

The dress tightened around her waist, hugged her ribs, squeezed her breasts.

"Bloody hell," Brendon said. "What have you been eating?"

"More to the point, what have your boobs been eating?" Georgie was staring at Megan's chest.

Megan looked down at her bust, which was struggling to stay contained in the bodice. "It's fine," she said, breathing in. "Is the zip up?"

"Yes, just." Brendon came to stand before her, next to Georgie.

"It fits okay," Megan said, adjusting the material over her chest.

"I did measure you right. I double checked, did it twice." Georgie frowned.

"You did. And the dress is great." So it's a fraction tight, what does it matter? It would probably stretch a little as she wore it.

Georgie and Brendon shared a look.

"What?" Megan asked.

"Nothing," Brendon said. He took her hands and held them out. "And I for one love it. You have a figure to die for and Georgie Porgy Pudding and Pie has hit the spot on what suits you."

Megan pushed down a wave of anxiety. She was pleased that a fuss wouldn't be made over the fit. She was just a bridesmaid. Georgie was the important one. As long as her dress was perfect, that was all that mattered.

She studied her reflection in the mirror again. Her boobs were bigger than usual. Am I putting on weight?

"Don't you dare say the F word," Georgie said. "Because it has no place here."

"But do you think—?"

"No." Georgie's face was stern. "That material has been cut a little off, is all."

"But you said she was one of the best—"

"We all make mistakes." Georgie ran her palm down Megan's arm. "You look amazing, all my single cousins are going to be chasing you."

"Except she's not available, is she?" Brendon said, holding up Megan's left hand.

"Oh, the ring, let me swoon over it in real life and not on a screen." Georgie clasped her hands over her cheeks. "Wow, it's lovely. It does have a bit of an antique vibe, doesn't it?"

"I think so," Megan said, pleasure combatting her worries over her dress. That was such a small detail when she had a wonderful, loving man to spend the rest of her life with.

As long as he's okay.

Her smile dropped.

"Now what?" Georgie asked, a concerned frown creasing her brow.

"I'm just so scared for him. Out there, in El Salvador."

"We know you are." Brendon rested his hand on her other shoulder.

"But he'll be all right," Georgie said, "I can feel it."

"What if he isn't? What if something has happened to him right now and I don't know about it? He could be hurt somewhere, being held hostage, a gun to his head or—"

"Stop. Stop. I'm not having this." Brendon waved her words away. "What good does all this what-if do anyone? Certainly not James and definitely not you."

"I agree with Brendon," Georgie said softly. "I get that you're scared, that you can't relax until he's home and you really, really wanted him here in London for the wedding. But you have to let him do his job and you have to get on with your life."

"I know." She sighed and blinked away a tear. "I'm sorry, you must be bored of me talking about it."

"Of course we're not. We're here to support you, help you."

"But creating crazy, nasty murderous scenarios in your head isn't conducive to your happiness, sweetpea," Brendon said. "So sometimes we have to be stern."

"I know, you're right." She admired her ring again. A flood of memories of James down on one knee, on the beach, drifted into her mind.

As did a conversation she'd had with her friends some time ago.

"Do you really like him?" she said.

"Who? James?" Georgie asked, surprise in her tone.

"Yes, James."

"Why on earth would you ask that?" Brendon shook his head. "I'd have thought it obvious that we do, very much."

"It's just…remember when I jilted Dylan?"

"As if we'd ever forget." Georgie folded her arms and tipped her head.

"And then afterwards, we were talking," Megan went on, "and you both said you'd never really liked him. I couldn't understand why you'd never told me. That his controlling, obsessive ways had never been mentioned."

"Because we thought you loved him. We didn't want to upset you," Georgie said.

"But I adore Tom and Zane." She turned to Brendon. "And if I didn't, if I thought they wouldn't complete you, make you as happy as you could be, then I'd say. So…"

"Do we like Hot Guy? Of course we do." Brendon reached for his drink and took a sip.

"Megan," Georgie said, "the thing with James is he doesn't try and change you. He loves you the way we do. You're not perfect, neither are we, neither is he, but that doesn't matter. Love is love with all its imperfections."

"And can you imagine growing old and grey together?"

Brendon asked.

Megan thought for a moment. James was handsome now. She imagined he'd just get more so with age. "Yes, definitely."

"With children and grandchildren all around you? Sitting on a swinging seat on a porch with a white picket fence?"

"I can." She nodded.

"Then all is perfect." Georgie gave her a hug.

"Well, it will be when he comes home…which will be soon," Brendon added.

Megan pulled in a deep breath. She'd been envious of what Georgie had with Tom. That soul-deep, life-long love, but now she had it with James and it felt good to love and to be loved.

"Be careful of that dress," Brendon said, "with all these hugs it will crease."

Georgie giggled and so did Megan as they broke apart.

"Anyway, enough of me," Megan said, glancing around the room. "Let me see the shoes I designed for you, Georgie. I worked on the prototype but haven't seen the end result."

"Oh, they're beautiful." Georgie's face lit up. "Hang on." She retrieved a pale blue box that had Winter Shoes stamped in silver on the lid.

Megan rubbed her hands together. These were bespoke. No one else had a pair—they were for Georgie and Georgie alone.

Brendon tugged the lid off with a lavish flick of his wrist. "Ta da."

Megan smiled and took one of the delicate cream heels from the box. The straps were whisper thin and dotted with tiny crystals, the inner sole was padded and naturally the base was sprinkled with glitter. "Do they fit okay?"

"Like a glove…well, a foot glove." Georgie laughed. "They're amazing, I can't thank you enough, and they're awesome with the dress, so delicate and pretty. Plus they're not going to cripple me as the day goes on."

"Good," Brendon said, "because although you'll end your

wedding day toppling into bed, the last thing we want is for you to be groaning about your sore feet."

9

"What do you think the next song will be?" Brendon asked, flopping into his seat and nudging the big cream bow that was tied around the back of the chair.

"If it's another sixties track I'm out of here." Megan laughed. "I know the older generation love it but I don't know the words."

"You and me both. Zane would, he's old before his years. A bit of Beach Boys or a rumble of The Monkees and he's off, no stopping those dancing feet of his."

"Are you missing him?" Megan pushed a plate of fancy little cakes across the table towards the elaborate rose centrepiece. She'd eaten more than enough and felt quite bloated.

"Naturally I'm missing him. He keeps me warm at night, like a sexy little hot water bottle," Brendon said, slugging on his red wine. "But this week in London will fly by and we'll be together again soon enough."

As will James and I.

She had to stay positive, keep her thoughts upbeat and manageable. Her friends had shown her that. What she'd do without them, she didn't know. They were her rock, her solid foundation, an anchor when life was a storm blustering around her.

"Aren't you going to dig into those cakes?" Brendon asked. "They look divine. So intricate."

"No, I'm full."

"Full? But you hardly touched your chicken or lemon torte." He frowned.

"I ate most of it." That wasn't quite true—the chicken had had too sweet a sauce coating it and the lemon had been slightly bitter. But she didn't want to say anything negative about the wedding breakfast at Georgie's amazing reception. It had all gone so smoothly, from church to fancy hotel, nothing untoward had happened, and the day had been a dreamboat of perfection which had showcased Georgie's flawless attention to detail and organisational skills.

The next song came on. But instead of another sixties track, it was a slow mellow tune.

"Ladies and gentleman," the DJ boomed, "please gather around as the bride and groom enjoy their first dance."

"Ah, how romantic, a sci-fi first dance." Brendon giggled. *"I Don't Want to Miss a Thing* always did give me that loving feeling."

"Come on, we should watch." Megan stood, adjusting the top of her dress as she did so. She'd reached the point where she'd be glad to get out of it and into her pyjamas.

Together they joined the crowd who'd circled Georgie and Tom. The disco lights flickered over the newlyweds, who'd embraced in the centre of the dance floor. They were swaying, locked together and gazing lovingly at each other.

Tom looked incredibly handsome in his sharp black morning suit, and Georgie's princess-style dress highlighted her enviable figure and elegant shoulders and arms. She'd taken her veil off, and the tiny crystals set in her hair sparkled in the flicker of the lights.

"They look so happy," Megan said, linking arms with Brendon.

"That's because they are. At some weddings," he said, "and once upon a time, when I was a betting man, I'd hedge bets on how long a newly hitched couple would last, but these two, they're keepers. They only have eyes for each other. I reckon they're in it for the long haul."

"Which is exactly how it should be."

"Damn right it is." He stroked his finger over her engagement ring. "So when will it be your big day?"

"I don't know. We haven't even talked about it."

"Will it be here or in LA?"

Megan shrugged. "Here, I suppose, but, yes, maybe LA... Oh, I don't know. With my parents and sister in Sydney and you and some of James' family in LA, I guess the USA would make sense."

"But have you even been to a church in LA?"

Tom twirled Georgie round and Megan caught a glimpse of her pretty shoes. "I'm ashamed to say no, I haven't."

"Oh well, that means you'll just have to get married on the beach then."

"Actually, that's not such a bad idea, and after all, he did propose on the beach so it would make sense."

"And it would save on the cost of a choir, bells, all that malarkey."

She gave his arm a squeeze. "Let me get James home safe first, then you can don your wedding planner hat again for me and wave your magic wand."

"Sweetpea, I have enough to be getting on with. Masterminding Winter Shoes' world domination is keeping me very busy, I'll have you know."

"Glad to hear it."

"Which reminds me, I got an email from Fanny Bailey earlier."

"Who?"

"Shame on you." He tutted. "Only the head shoe buyer for Harrods. She is the Queen of Sole, get it?"

"I do." She smiled. "And...more importantly, what did she have to say?"

"We've got an appointment with her on Tuesday about shelf space."

"That's great news." And it really was. Exactly what Megan had been hoping for. And to get the appointment while they were already in town was a double bonus. Making another trip back just for one meeting would have been a pain.

"I've already set Enid on the case. Said we'd be in the Change Street office on Monday to finalise."

"Good plan."

The song came to an end. Georgie and Tom concluded their first dance with a long kiss that had someone shouting at them to come up for air.

Megan ran her hand over her stomach. It was gurgling. She was hot, too. The room had become very stuffy.

"I might just nip to the ladies'," she said to Brendon.

"You okay?" He looked at her holding her stomach.

"Yeah, just feeling a bit…"

"Sick?"

She nodded. "Back in a minute."

Weaving through the crowd, who were milling back to their seats, Megan took deep breaths. The last thing she wanted was to be sick out here. She had to get to the restroom.

There was a waiter in her way, then an older lady with a stick, but eventually she pushed into the quiet ladies' toilets.

A torrent of nausea gripped her and she leaned over the bowl. Her skin tingled, her hair made her scalp hot and the dress gripped her like a fist. But luckily nothing came of it. She didn't vomit and after a few minutes she headed for the sink. Placing her wrists beneath cold running water, she tried to compose herself.

Worrying about James was manifesting itself in all kinds of ways. Putting on weight by comfort eating, feeling exhausted and now nausea washing over her at the most inconvenient of times.

There was a sudden knock on the door.

Megan glanced at it.

Who knocks on restroom doors?

"Megan?"

"Brendon?"

"Can I come in?" He poked his head into the room.

"Yes."

"Is there anyone else in here?"

"No."

"Good, I don't want to scare the heebie-jeebies out of

some poor old dear."

"It's empty." She turned off the water. "What's up?"

"You."

"What about me?"

He cocked one eyebrow. "You, my darling, dearest, naïve friend, need to do something."

"And what would that be?" She was confused by his suddenly determined expression.

"You need to go pee on this." He held out a slim white box that had *Clear Blue* written on the side.

"What...what's that? Why have you—"

"Oh come on, Megan." He bumped the heel of his palm against his forehead. "You're sick, tired, big-bloody-boobs, do the maths. You went to sex-ed at school, right?"

She stared at the box. *Pregnant? Me? A baby? James' baby?*

The nausea welled again and she swallowed rapidly, circling her throat with her fingers.

"Either you have a bun in the oven or you've got one nasty bug, and I know which way I'm betting."

"I thought you weren't a betting man anymore." She frowned.

"For this I'll make an exception, the odds are pretty damn good." He thrust the box farther forwards.

Megan took it.

"Go, go forth and pee." He flapped his hand at a cubicle.

Megan suddenly felt like she was floating. Everything slightly out of focus. The room smelt strongly of cleaning fluid and the lights were too bright. But she did as she'd been instructed and headed into the loo, which had walnut-effect wall panelling and a bowl of raspberry-coloured potpourri on a little shelf behind the cistern.

She wriggled and jigged, tugging up the tight-fitting dress, then pulled the small white wand from the box.

What the hell will I do if I'm pregnant?

Thoughts collided in her brain. *Will James be happy? Will I be happy? What will it mean to my business? Winter Shoes, my TV profile—it's all hotting up, but with a baby in the middle of all of this…*

"Come on, girl, get on with it," Brendon called through the door.

"I am."

"What's going on?"

Megan heard Georgie's voice.

"She's in there," Brendon said.

"Oh… I was looking for her. My hair is coming down at the back, some of the pins are loose."

"I'll do that for you. Turn around."

Megan could feel her heart pounding. She was a little breathless, too.

"Why are you in here, Brendon?" Georgie asked.

"Because I'm waiting for her to do something."

"You are?"

"Yes, I've just instructed our little shoe designer to go pee on a preggers stick."

"Oh, thank goodness for that," Georgie said.

There was a bang on the door. "Megan, I'm here," Georgie said. "Come out as soon as you've done it."

Megan opened the door. The small white object that would decide her fate was held at her side.

"Oh, sweetie, it will all be okay." Georgie pulled Megan into a hug. Brendon moved with her, still fiddling with her hair.

"Of course it will," Brendon said. "A little baby James or a little baby Megan will be absolutely adorable in all of our lives. And I for one can't wait to be an uncle."

"Can we just, you know, see what the test says?" Megan said, studying Georgie's face.

"It really will be okay, whatever the result." Georgie held her cheeks. "I promise."

Megan knew she couldn't really promise that, but it was good to hear. She glanced at the tiny screen—one blue line. "It's negative. Positive is two lines."

"Hold your horses." Brendon picked up the box. "It takes a few minutes."

"Did you know he'd bought this?" Megan asked Georgie.

"Yes." She nodded. "After yesterday, the dress." She indicated Megan's generous cleavage. "The sickness, the tears..."

"Bloody hell." It all fell into place. What Megan had been dismissing as worry and jetlag came together like a jigsaw. She'd been blind to it. Not seeing what was under her nose. *How could I be so dumb?* "I'm pregnant," she said. "I know I am. I can feel it. My body feels different, not quite mine."

"And that's where you're right." Brendon took the stick from her and held it up. "It now belongs to a baby, too."

He flashed the screen that contained two blue lines her way.

Silence.

Georgie gripped Megan's hand.

Brendon was shaking, the stick jiggling slightly, and he was breathing fast.

Megan stared into the mirror, at her neat, flat abdomen. There was a baby in there. A tiny little person that she and James had made. It felt unreal but at the same time so real.

The future flashed before her—a large swollen belly, childbirth, a babe in her arms, a toddler beside her. James pushing a pram, changing a nappy, playing football with a son, driving a daughter to ballet classes.

It was a beautiful future, full of love and laughter and togetherness.

As sudden as the shock of finding out she was pregnant had been, the sense of it being right was also quick to descend upon her.

She looked at Georgie. "I'm going to be a mother."

"You are. And a wonderful one." She smiled, her eyes misting with emotion.

"Congratu-bloody-lations!" Brendon said, his eyes wide. "I can hardly believe it."

"Of course you can, you bought the test. You were the first to know," Megan said.

"I suppose so." He laughed, a rather hysterical bubble of

noise. "And they're not cheap, you know, those tests, and I bought four in case we had a dodgy one."

"I'll pay you back." She paused. "What is James going to say?"

"Call him?" Georgie said, brushing a crease from her bridal gown.

"What, now?"

"Yes, now," she said.

"But." Megan shook her head. "No, this is your day, Georgie. Let's put this to one side and I'll call him tomorrow." She indicated the door. "We should get back out there and party."

"The hell we should, you're a pregnant woman, we need to let the father of your child know that he's expecting."

Despite her joy and the unexpected news, a flutter of sadness drifted through her. "But he's so hard to contact. I've tried a couple of times and it just goes to voicemail. I'll have to wait for him to call me when he gets to a landline. If he gets to a landline."

"You have to at least try." Georgie held her hand out to Brendon.

He pulled both of their phones from the breast pocket of his jacket and handed Megan's over.

"Tom will wonder where you are," Megan said. "You should go and find him."

"Tom is going to be at my side for the rest of my life, he'll wait a few minutes while we sort this out." She tapped the screen of the phone. "What's your password?"

"Three, three, five, five."

She tapped it in, her finger flying over the screen. "Ah, here we go, James." She handed the phone to Megan.

She pressed it to her ear, and as she did so a coil of anxiety wrapped around her chest. It was ringing loud and clear. If only she knew if he could hear it. Was it in his pocket? A bag? A hotel room? Was the battery flat? She had no idea. All she knew was she wanted him, so desperately, to answer.

To hear his familiar deep voice now would make everything right. It would make it real. She ached for him. Her heart rate sped up and her throat felt tight. "James," she whispered.

"Is he there?" Georgie asked hopefully.

Megan shook her head. "No."

The phone went to a female voice telling her the call could not be connected. She hung up as tears stabbed at her eyes. It didn't seem right to impart such monumental news as a message. What she wanted most was to tell him in person. See his eyes, his expression. Know that he was happy about it, too.

And for that she'd have to wait.

She just hoped she'd get the chance to tell him. That he wasn't lying dead in a gutter somewhere, rats and snakes and…

A sob bubbled up and she pressed her hand to her mouth.

"Come on, sit down, take the weight off your feet," Brendon said, dragging a chair to the middle of the restroom. "There's the baby to think of now. Don't get yourself all in a dither again."

Megan did as he'd asked.

"And just because he didn't answer doesn't mean he's not okay," Georgie said as if reading her mind. "He told you that, didn't he, before he went? Phone calls would be hard."

Megan nodded. "Yes. He did."

"So, no tears, this is a happy day, I'm married and you're having a baby." Georgie knelt and put her hands on Megan's knees, the wide dress she wore puffing up around her. "We'll talk about this for years to come. A red-letter day for both of us."

"I know." Megan was quiet. "A baby."

"Yes, a baby." Brendon clapped. "Best day ever. I wish Zane was here to enjoy this."

The door opened and a woman in a pretty dress and a large hat walked in.

"Mum," Georgie said, standing.

"Jean, how are you?" Brendon beamed, almost hopping on the spot. "You're just in time."

"What's going on? Why are you in the ladies' restroom, Brendon?" Jean looked around the room. Her gaze fell on the pregnancy test that Brendon had placed by a sink. "Is that what I think it is?"

"Er, yes, actually it is." Brendon waved it in the air then set it down again. "And come to mention it, now is a really good time for me to depart. I shouldn't be in here, you're right. To-da-loo."

He slipped from the room, the noise of the disco loud for a moment as the door was open then quiet descended as it fell shut.

"Well," Jean said, her attention on Georgie. "Had you planned on telling me today?"

"Telling you what?" Georgie stood with a confused frown on her face.

"That I'm going to be a grandmother."

"Oh, Mum." Georgie rushed to her and took her hands. "Hopefully one day, but not yet."

Jean frowned. "I don't…understand."

"It's Megan. Megan is expecting." Georgie gestured to Megan.

"Oh…well, congratulations, how exciting." Jean rushed up to Megan and took her hand. "How far along are you?"

"Not very." Megan hadn't even thought about that. She would have to, though, when her head cleared a little. Work out dates and figure out when she'd need to have a nursery ready by and little clothes and nappies and…

"I'm so thrilled for you. Of course I would have loved to meet your fiancé today—Georgie has told me what a fine man he is," Jean was saying. "And I hope we'll get to meet him soon. It's so lovely that all you girls—and boys—have found partners. It makes me so happy. Love is the one true thing we must all search for and having a child with the man of your dreams is the icing on the cake."

"Thank you, Jean." Megan smiled. "I think I'll just feel

better when I've told him."

"He doesn't know?" She looked surprised.

"Not yet," Georgie said. "He's in the jungle, fighting drug warlords and seeking justice for the world's poor."

10

James

James gripped the scratchy rope and kept his gaze straight ahead. Looking down would be a mistake, he knew that. It would throw what tiny semblance of self-control he had out of the window. Heights had never been his thing, and walking over safe, solid bridges spanning ordinary rivers made his head fuzzy, so this decrepit old thing straddling a torrential tributary of the Rio Lempa had his adrenaline working overtime and his imagination on full throttle.

"It's okay," Grant called from several steps ahead. He was already striding across the flimsy structure. "Come on. You'll be fine. It's quite stable, really."

James studied the old, worn slats precariously secured at either end to the ropes that seemed to be the main component of the bridge. They were haphazard—clearly some had broken loose and fallen to the gushing river below. He pulled in a deep breath. He had to do this. Even though at their widest the slats were a large stride apart and left no room for error.

Grant didn't seem fazed and, holding on to the two lengths of rope that acted as handrails, he was powering forwards—his equipment on his back—and had nearly reached the other side. For a moment, James felt jealous of his mate's confidence. Soon Grant would be over this churning river that divided one territory from another, each controlled by a different drug gang. But then he remembered how Grant had screamed when a bat had fluttered by his head the night before. Bats, it seemed, were his cameraman's weakness. Which was ridiculous. Bats wouldn't exactly kill him, but falling fifty feet into a raging surge of water that was littered with boulders as big as a car—now that was considerably more lethal.

"We should get a move on," Brent said, his voice gruff. He was the older of the two US ex-military guys James had hired to travel with them and, hopefully, keep them as safe as it was possible to be. "We need to make camp before nightfall and it will be dusk in three hours."

"I'm not sure about this bridge," James said, still hesitating.

"It's been here for decades, it's not going to break now."

It might.

"And we have no choice," Brent went on. "This is our only way forward if you want to get to Tecoluca tomorrow."

"I know." He nodded, summoning his courage. He wondered what the hell Megan would say if she could see him now. It didn't bear thinking about.

"Come on, the others are waiting." Brent dropped some of the sternness from his voice. "And I'll be right behind you. We'll do this together."

"Okay." James steeled himself. He had no choice but to cross to the other side. And Brent was right—the bridge had been spanning this river for a long time. All he had to do was stay calm and walk in the same footsteps Grant had just done.

He took a tentative step farther onto it, wishing his stomach wasn't doing somersaults.

"Come on, won't take long," Grant called. He'd reached the other side now and stood watching him with Luca, their other hired protection who was also, conveniently, of Central American descent.

James set off. His plan of not looking down was impossible because he had to carefully check where he put each foot. The best he could do was try to block out the snarling water below and not to let the roar of it colliding with rocks and crashing into the cliffs either side get to him.

He thought of Megan, and her pretty smile, and the fact that she was waiting for him when he got out of this hellhole. He longed to spend a night in a proper bed with her, instead of what he'd become used to—an uncomfortable night on the forest floor with only the creepy crawlies and three not very pleasant-smelling men for company. Not that he was smelling of flowers. A shower wouldn't go amiss. And some fresh clothes. *Mmm, a shower with Megan, now that I can cope with.*

"That's it, you're half way," Brent said. "Keep at it. Keep going."

A sudden trill ringing punctuated the air, managing to make itself heard over the thunderous noise below. James was aware of vibrating against his chest, right over his heart.

His phone was ringing.

"Ignore it?" Brent said.

James didn't even bother to answer Brent. He wasn't letting go of the ropes—he was gripping so hard his knuckles had whitened—for anything. Least of all his phone.

But what if it was Megan? They'd been out of contact for what felt like forever, though the truth was it had only been a few weeks. He didn't want to miss the chance to speak to her.

A strange feeling went through him. A sensation of certainty. It was Megan calling, he was sure of it. He would put good money on it. They were so in tune, so connected, he could imagine her sitting on the other side of the world, in London with her friends, holding the phone to her ear. She'd be pensive, worried, likely just ringing on the off chance he had a signal, which for a change, he did.

He paused, feeling the rope bridge swaying beneath his feet and his palms. He locked his elbows and knees. Could he risk it? Let go for a moment and answer the call? What he wouldn't give to hear her sweet voice right now. His fiancée, the woman of his dreams. He wished she were with him.

No, scrap that, he'd never want her in this much danger or in this war-torn, corrupt country. For all its natural beauty, it wasn't somewhere he'd ever want any of his family to find themselves.

On and on the phone rang.

He lifted his right hand from the rope.

Immediately his balance went off kilter. He gasped and clutched it again.

"What the fuck are you doing?" Brent shouted from behind him. "There are some moments in life, mate, when it's just not convenient to answer your damn cell."

James knew Brent was right. Now was not the time to try to speak to Megan. Apart from anything else she'd hear the fear in his voice and be all the more worried. He'd try to call her back, when he got to the other side of the bridge, and hope that he still had a signal there.

"I know, I know," he muttered, taking another step. "I wasn't going to answer it."

The ringing stopped.

He missed it. For a moment Megan had been with him—not that she wasn't always in his heart and thoughts—but to feel her call, against his flesh, that had been special.

He pushed on, getting more confident once he'd gone past the halfway mark and the slats were closer together.

"Nearly done it," Grant called.

James noticed that he was rolling the camera, getting footage of James navigating the primitive bridge. It might come in useful as a filler. James loved that about Grant. He never missed an opportunity, was always a step ahead and thinking about the end product and how it would look on screen. He was more than a cameraman, he saw the big picture and was a talent in the industry. James knew he was lucky to have him.

Finally, James hit solid land. He blew out a breath and flexed and unflexed his fingers. His hands had cramped from holding on so tightly.

"You've gone a bit pale, mate," Grant said with a chuckle.

"I can think of better ways to spend an afternoon," James muttered.

Brent stepped up behind him, compass in hand. "We go

west for a few miles, then I recommend we hunker down for the night."

"Suits me," James said, pulling out his phone. His heart swelled. He had a missed call from Megan. He'd *known* it was her. Every sense and instinct in his body had screamed that it had been her.

Quickly he hit return call and held it to his ear.

Grant gave him a quizzical look.

"Megan, she tried to call when I was halfway across." James rolled his eyes. "Handy, eh?"

"Wow, you had a signal." Grant appeared impressed. "Is it ringing?"

"No." James frowned. There was nothing, no sound. He glanced at the screen. He had one bar of reception. "Mmm... I'll try again."

He did, but this time the phone switched off completely. "Oh, bloody hell," he said, a weight tugging at his stomach. "Now I'm out of battery."

"It lasted longer than mine." Grant shrugged. "I'd just sent a text to a mate in LA to update him on our near run in with that cartel up north and then that was it, dead."

"If only I'd..."

"Answered your phone on the bridge," Brent said, wiping his forearm over his sweaty brow. "You wouldn't be here now. That bridge is a two-hand job."

"Yeah, not worth taking a dive for the sake of a call," Grant agreed.

James looked back out at the bridge. Had she just been calling to see if he was okay? Maybe she'd just wanted a chat, to hear his voice the same way he wanted to hear hers. Was she all right? It was Georgie's wedding about now—he wasn't sure of the days exactly. Had the celebrations gone well?

"This way," Luca said, using a machete to hack aside a few long tendrils. "It's not a path and it will be slow going, but it looks navigable."

James slipped his phone away then, slugging from his

water bottle, set off after Luca. Grant and Brent followed.

They battled on through the undergrowth and up and down several steep banks. James spotted small and large snakes, but the creatures were in a rush to get away from the four men marching through their space so he took little notice of them. It was the same with the insects – he'd become accustomed to them buzzing about, though he was still fascinated by some of the alien-like creepy-crawlies he'd come across. Nature really excelled in the unusual in the jungle.

By the time they'd been going for an hour, the bridge and his phone call from Megan were a distant memory. Spider monkeys chattered in the branches around him and he caught sight of several flashes of blue and red in the trees above – macaws, Brent had told him a few days previously.

As they rounded a bend on the side of a mountainous cliff, Luca held up his hand and stopped walking. "Halt."

James came to an abrupt standstill, as did the two men behind him. He then stood shoulder to shoulder with Luca and looked down into the small valley below.

A tin hut with only one wall and a roof stood amongst patches of maize, cassava and strips of cocoa. The cocoa appeared innocuous, almost like young coffee plants, with its soft green foliage. If James hadn't familiarised himself with it, he'd never have known what it was.

"It's a smallholding, likely cultivated by a peasant family in the area," James said quietly. "But controlled by one of the gangs ruling over this territory."

"Is there anyone about?" Grant asked.

"No, not that I can see," Brent whispered. "You wait here. I'll do a recce. No one move until I get back."

He slipped off to the right, moving silently, and almost at once was lost to the jungle.

"You heard what he said. We wait," Luca muttered. "Keep quiet."

Grant was shifting behind him, getting the camera ready. "This would make for a great at camera narration," he said quietly to James.

"Let's just see what Brent comes up with," James replied. For all they knew, the farmer, likely armed, was hanging around, or worse still, his boss and henchmen. Coming face to face with a bunch of angry drug producers with AK47s wasn't something he wanted to cope with after the day they'd had marching through forestation. In fact, he didn't fancy it any day, come to think of it.

After ten minutes Brent reappeared, joining them from the left. "I've done a loop, there's nothing going on. A fire was lit, possibly yesterday or the day before, and there's evidence of a place where someone sleeps on occasion, but it's deserted at the moment."

"It's obviously just been left to grow and they'll use that hut for harvest and manufacture when it's ripe." James studied the area.

"I'm no expert," Luca said, "but I reckon that's got another month of growing before it's ready for picking."

"So do you think we can go down there, take a look?" James asked. "Will it be safe?"

Luca huffed. "If it were up to me I'd give it a wide berth, but so far you guys seem intent on ticking all the danger boxes." He shrugged. "So do what you want."

"Yeah, have at it," Brent said, "we'll keep lookout. One word from us, though, and you're back here, this spot, no questions, got it?"

"Roger that," James said. A thrill went through him. This would make for some great footage—the very heart of the problem, the place where it all started. The farmer's field, the cocaine factory.

They headed to the hut and, after a few minutes of looking around at the various primitive tools and implements that were lying in wait for the harvest, Grant held up the camera. "You ready?" he asked.

"Yep." James plucked the top leaves off a cocoa plant to his right and stared at the lens.

Grant gave him the signal.

"This plant appears harmless," he said, holding up the foliage, "almost pretty, but if you believe that it's never done any damage you'd be sorely mistaken. Because these cocoa leaves are converted into cocaine and what was once a leafy shrub growing lazily in the jungle goes on to leave death and devastation in its wake. And that trail of carnage starts right here, with the impoverished farmers who tend these jungle-hidden crop fields. Once these poor families produced coffee for the world, earned an honest income, but now they're ordered by ruthless gangs to grow cocoa.

"So what is the government doing about it? The International Narcotics Control Board, the INCB, are taking it seriously, but what's needed is the rest of the world to also sit up and take notice. And I believe that starts with putting it right, fixing it here, with the farmer, at grass root level." He dropped the leaves to the ground and crushed them with his foot. "These farmers need to have protection from the unscrupulous bullies who threaten not just their livelihoods but their lives, and their families' lives, too. If they do not produce a certain tonnage of cocaine each year, they must face the consequences of the corrupt gangs who roam the area claiming it as their own. And let me tell you, from what we've heard, those consequences are bloody and wicked.

"The US, Canada and Mexico are the biggest customers and it's time the people in power took a look at what's growing in their next-door neighbour's garden and woke up to the reality." He paused for effect, then, "Just how many more people, innocent people, men, women and children, have got to die before that happens?"

He turned and walked into the shade of the hut.

Grant let the camera roll for another few seconds then lowered it. "I think you'll be pleased with that, boss," he said, grinning.

"It's certainly the kind of place we wanted to find." James stepped into the blazing sun again. "Full of atmosphere."

"Hey, guys, let's get out of here," Brent called. "Don't

want to push our luck."

"He's right," James said. "I can't imagine this kind of place is left unattended for long."

"Yeah, we were lucky to get it for a few minutes."

They headed back into the darkness and relative safety of the jungle. Both Brent and Luca had guns out and wore deadly serious expressions as they scanned their location.

"You okay?" James asked them.

"Gut feeling," Luca muttered. "We're out of here, now."

"Fine by me." James glanced over his shoulder. Everything was as they'd left it a few minutes before. The sun still poured down, the crop swayed gently in the breeze and small birds busied about. But he couldn't help feeling that Luca was right—it was time to get away from this place.

As they headed stealthily through the undergrowth, still moving west, James wondered at how his sixth senses always became heightened when he was in this kind of situation. It had happened in the Middle East, too. He'd had a feeling when things were about to go wrong, or when he had to get the hell out of the situation he was in. He'd had a few close calls, yes, but thank goodness that was all they'd been—near misses.

They marched for another hour then came across a small spring that collected in a deep pool before trickling over a makeshift rocky dam and into the dark forest.

"This should do us for the night," Grant said, looking at the moss-covered clearing that stretched in a triangular shape from the bubbling water. "What do you think?"

"Perfect, and yes, it's time to call it a day," James said, letting his rucksack fall to the ground. Without the weight of it on his shoulders, he felt light.

"Time for a dip," Brent said, grinning suddenly.

It was the first time James had seen him produce a proper smile. "A dip?"

"Yeah, I'm going in. Smelling like a sewer rat has lost its novelty and this looks considerably more inviting than those other leech-infested pools we've come across." Within a few seconds he'd stripped to his boxers and jumped in. The splash covered James, Grant and Luca.

They all laughed.

"How's the water?" Luca asked with a chuckle.

"Perfect." Brent shook his head, water flicking from his hair.

"I think it's time we all ditched this sewer rat cologne." Grant tugged at his T-shirt.

"I couldn't agree more," James said, pulling at his boots. "And Mother Nature has provided."

11

Megan

It had been hot in London but it was hotter back in LA. Megan found the heat really didn't help her nausea or exhaustion. The tiredness she was feeling wasn't like having a few sleepless nights or jetlag, it was to-the-bone tired, brain-not-working tired, and the only thing for it was to give in to it and go to bed.

Brendon had taken to spending a lot of his time at James' beach house with her, insisting she needed to be kept an eye on. Megan didn't think she did but was happy to have Brendon around. He kept her mind off the gnawing worries she had about James and he always seemed to think up tasty little morsels for her to nibble on at just the right moment. He was equally easy-going if she took one look at a meal and pushed it away.

"So what are you wearing for your next slot on *Lavinia Heats It Up?*" Brendon asked. "I know you had two dresses in mind but we need to make a decision and get our butts to the studio."

Megan glanced at the clock on the wall. She was sprawled on the sofa in a T-shirt and cotton shorts and the doors to the balcony were open, the breeze covering her in soft ocean scents every few seconds. "Is it that time already?"

"I'm afraid it is, Hot Momma. We need to shake our booties and get this show on the road."

She shut her eyes and tipped her head to the ceiling. The sea air was soothing, she'd found, one of the few smells that didn't make her heave in the morning. Luckily by this time of day the sickness was easing off and it was just the fatigue that plagued her.

"Come on, come on." Brendon clapped, the noise ringing around the house. "I know you're growing another human being and all that, but the TV studio will wait for no one."

Megan groaned and pushed herself into a sitting position, pausing for a moment to check she wasn't going to go light-headed or be attacked by a wave of bile.

All was good.

She opened her eyes and stood. "Okay, okay. I'm up."

Brendon pulled a face. "Blimey, makeup have got their work cut out today."

"Hey, thanks for that." She frowned.

"Oh, you know, it's just the pallor, white with a hint of apple-green."

Megan's frowned deepened.

"But a coating of foundation and a hefty dollop of bronzer and you'll be perfectly acceptable."

Megan sighed. "Let's hope they work magic."

"Of course they do. It's what they're paid for." He held up two dresses. One was pale pink with white polka dots and would go with her pearlescent shell-inspired sandals, and the other was more formal, a russet-red and very fitted. She'd planned on teaming that with killer velvet heels. "Which one?"

"The pink, it's looser. I can't stand anything tight around my waist."

"But you haven't even got a bump. Not even a pimple-sized bump."

"I know, it's just how it feels, you know."

"No, I don't know, and thank the good Lord above I'll never be held hostage by a tadpole-sized human, no offence."

"None taken."

He dumped the red dress over the nearest chair. "Are you getting changed here or there?"

"There, just in case I puke in the car."

"Are you feeling that bad?"

"No, not really. I'll be fine." She grinned suddenly. "Let's just be glad it's a late-night show and not an early morning one, eh?"

"Yeah, otherwise the viewers would learn a bit more about you than your shoe savvy, and I'm sure they'd rather not be privy to the contents of your stomach."

Megan ambled into the kitchen and sipped a glass of water. She then headed into the bedroom and pulled on loose sweats and soft pumps. "Come on, let's hit the road," she said, wandering into the lounge.

"Yes, Miss."

Within half an hour they were in the studios. Megan flipped through the script that she'd been involved in writing over the last few days. She was being joined on Lavinia's show by the Hollywood gossip blogger, Nina Charles, and they had some good lines to bounce off each other.

"Where is Nina?" Brendon asked, wringing his hands together and glancing about.

"No idea." Megan tilted her chin as the makeup girl applied her usual red lipstick.

Brendon paced to the right, then the left, his shiny neon blue shoes clicking on the floor. He rubbed his palms on his super-skinny black jeans then fiddled with the navy paisley print silk shirt that hugged his slender torso.

"Chill out," Megan said.

"But you'll be stuck without her. You can't sit and gossip on your own for half an hour."

"It will be fine."

"No, I'm not sure it will be, she should be here by now." He glanced in the mirror and fussed with the tips of his carefully styled hair. "Maybe I should go and find Larry, the producer, see what's going on."

"If that would make you feel better, go for it." Megan squeezed her lips together on a bit of tissue to blot the lipstick.

"I will, I'll be back in a mo." He dashed from the room, the door slamming behind him.

"He's a live wire," the makeup girl commented.

"Tell me about it, he makes me dizzy sometimes." Megan laughed. "I couldn't cope without him, though."

"Yeah, he seems a good sort, your best interests at heart. You need people like that around you in this crazy city."

"It does seem that way."

Suddenly the door burst open.

Brendon shot in, waving his hands above his head. "She's a no-show. A bloody no-show. The little tart has let us down!"

"What?" Megan jumped up from the seat.

The makeup girl retreated, mascara wand held aloft.

"How am I supposed to talk to myself?" Megan's head was spinning. She pressed her fingertips to her temples. "Can they get Lavinia back?"

"No, of course not, she's sunning herself in Indian Wells." Brendon whirled on the spot, his arms fluttering like a panicked butterfly.

"Why don't you go on?" the makeup girl said, waving her mascara wand at Brendon.

"Me?" Brendon stared at her.

"Yes, you, Brendon. You look the part, from what I've seen you've got the lines as rehearsed as Megan has and well…" She paused. "The viewing masses will go wild for your cute English accent."

Brendon's mouth fell open.

Megan held back a giggle. Seeing him speechless was a rarity and a treat. "I think it's a great idea."

"No." Brendon shook his head. "No, I don't think so. And besides, Larry would never go for it. I haven't got any experience on screen and, and…"

"Who said I wouldn't go for it?" Larry's deep voice boomed into the room.

Brendon twirled around, his fingers tapping repeatedly on his lips. "Oh, there you are."

"Yes, here I am, and I think it's an excellent idea. Get yourself ready, Brendon, we need you." He clamped his big hand on Brendon's shoulder.

Brendon staggered slightly and a flush of colour attacked his cheeks. "Well, if you think..."

"I do think," Larry said firmly. "It's a perfect solution, and Skye here is right, the audience will love you and your accent. The whole package, in fact."

"And there's no one more qualified to sit up there with me and chat about shoe choices of the rich and famous, and what's new and what's hot," Megan said, reaching for his hands. "Please say you'll do it."

He stared at her, his eyes wide.

"I need you," she said. "Again."

He pulled in a deep breath and gave a sharp nod. "Yes, I will answer this hour of need and step in. It is my duty as a shoe guru. I owe it to the world of fashionistas and the slaves of trend."

He was tugged sideways by Skye, the makeup girl. "Sit, we haven't got long."

Brendon's bum landed in the chair Megan had just vacated. "Oh, okay. Yes, do it. Make me camera ready." He wafted his hand in the air. "Work your magic."

Megan blew out a breath. That had been a close call. Thank goodness for Brendon. It would be a breeze with him—they could talk shoes all day, and frequently did—doing it on air wouldn't be any different.

Or so she hoped.

"You okay with this plan?" Larry asked her.

"Absolutely." She paused. "As long as you think Lavinia will be, too."

"Hah, Lavinia." He batted his hand in front of his face as though swatting a fly. "When she's off on holiday, and leaves—no offence—a couple of inexperienced hosts, she'll have to suck up the solutions we find when there's a no-show." He reached for the door handle. "But you'll be great, you were a natural last time. Now get a move on, you've got twenty minutes till I need you on set."

"I'll be there."

He left and Megan slipped her dress on. It had been the right choice and was floaty and soft on her skin. She added a chunky necklace and straightened her beloved engagement ring.

"Where are the shoes that go with this?" she asked Brendon.

"In that bag there." He gestured to a red holdall beneath a dressing table.

Megan pulled a box out and flipped the lid. The shoes nestled inside were one of her favourite summer designs. The straps were delicate and pearlescent and the heel was high. As with all her shoes, the inner soles were cushioned so they'd be perfectly comfortable.

She sat and set about putting them on. For some reason they were a bit tight, not quite right over her toes and where the strap buckled at her ankle. She checked the size. They were her shoes *and* the correct size.

She stood and stared down at her toes. Her nails were painted in a French polish and her skin held a light tan. But the flesh around the straps…she'd swear it was puffy and it certainly felt like the straps were digging in.

"Oh no!" she cried.

"What?" Brendon asked, studying her reflection in the mirror. "What the heavens above is it that's got you screaming like a banshee?"

"I've got fat feet," Megan wailed.

"No you haven't." He turned the chair around, Skye following him with her blusher brush.

"I have. You can't deny it."

He stared at her feet. "No you haven't."

"I have, really." She stomped up to him. "They resemble slabs of meat strung up with butcher's string."

"Now you're just being dramatic." He tutted.

"They look fine to me," Skye said, bending to study Megan's feet.

Megan ran her hands over her waist and blinked rapidly. The urge to cry had washed over her. *Fat feet, whatever next?*

"Besides, you're not far enough along to get swelling," Brendon said. "That's for your third trimester."

"How do you know?" Megan asked.

He shrugged. "I've been reading *Get Clued Up When You Get Knocked Up*, it's got all the information you need."

"That's a real book?" Megan asked.

"Oh, are you expecting?" Skye asked, grinning broadly.

Megan automatically ran her hand over her stomach. "Yes. But I'm keeping it quiet for now."

Skye did a zipper motion over her lips. "Your secret is safe with me."

"Thanks."

She studied Megan's feet again. "Really, they're fine, nothing pregnant about them."

"Do you really think?" Megan checked the glitter on the soles.

"You have very pretty feet and very pretty shoes." Skye smiled and set the brush she was holding aside. "And that's me done, so you two had better go and kill it."

Brendon sprang to his feet. "Yes, don't want to be late for the Megan and Brendon show." He grabbed Megan's hand. "Come on, let's hit the studio."

"Thank you for watching *Lavinia Heats It Up*, you've been great." Megan beamed at the camera that had the small red light on the top. "And until next time, keep your dancing shoes on, no matter what you're doing. Lavinia will be back on the couch next week to bring you up to date on what's trending in Italy and how the stars' wardrobes fared at Maximillion and Cashmere's wedding in Thailand."

"And that's a thank you from me, too, Brendon Trugate. See you next time. Be hot when you need to be and cool when the temperature gets too much." Brendon waved at the camera, his face a picture of glee.

Larry did a three, two, one sign with his fingers then drew a line across his throat. "That's a wrap, we're off air."

"Phew," Megan said. "You okay?"

"I'm fine." Brendon was all but bouncing up and down on the seat. "That was incredible. I loved it, every moment. Can we do it again?"

Larry stepped up them.

Behind him the small audience were standing and beginning to shuffle from the studio.

"You two did great," he said, "not a word out of place."

"I'm pleased you're pleased," Brendon said, getting to his feet.

Megan reached for her glass of water and took a sip. The slot had gone really well. She was getting used to this television business and, like Brendon, had enjoyed herself.

"Better than some of the so-called professionals around here," Larry said, "and it's refreshing to have the bitching off the menu. I know it pulls viewers in and it will be dish of the day next week when Lavinia is back, but you two were all about the shoes."

"Well it was a special shoe edition," Megan said with a smile as she stood.

"And you pulled it off." He glanced at his watch. "I have to go, but this isn't goodbye, I'll see you both again, on set. You've been stars in your own right."

"Thanks, Larry." Brendon stood and held out his hand. "For believing in me."

"Ah, you believed in yourself." Larry shook then slapped Brendon on the shoulder.

Brendon staggered slightly but his smile didn't falter.

"And it paid off," Larry said. "See you kids around."

Brendon turned to Megan and pulled her into a hug. "Do you think he'll give us our own show? I can see it now, pink glitter writing over a rainbow shoe, *The Megan and Brendon Show* or *Megan and Brendon Do Over LA.*"

"I think that might be stretching it a bit too far."

"Well you never know." He released her. "And if you don't hitch your wagon to the stars you'll never get there, will you?"

"True." She lifted a pile of papers that had been out of sight and had a quick glance through them. They'd covered everything she'd wanted to, including a few plugs for Winter Shoes.

As she skimmed over her sprawling handwriting, a conversation nearby caught her attention.

It was two of the cameramen, chatting as they shut down their equipment.

"You heard from your mad buddy who's filming in El Salvador?" one said.

"Grant?" the other asked.

"Yeah, that's him."

"Actually, I did. He sent me a text when he had a rare bit of signal."

"How's it going out there in the jungle?"

"They had a run-in with a cartel up north. And I'm guessing those guys weren't pleased at having a documentary made about them."

"Not surprising, and damn, I wouldn't want to get on their wrong side."

"Me neither. I can imagine it gets pretty tense out there, what with scared farmers who also have guns thrown into the mix. I bet Grant is beginning to wonder why the hell he went."

A bitter taste rose in Megan's mouth, coating her throat and tongue. She swallowed it down, hoping she wouldn't vomit. They had to be talking about Grant and James—how many other Grants were there in El Salvador shooting that exact type of footage?

She looked at Brendon.

He was staring at her, his mouth a straight line, clearly also listening to what was being said.

"I don't know why he did go. I mean, I'm all for edgy documentaries but there's edgy and then there's crazy. A couple of white Americans would be worth a lot of money in ransom."

"Must be worth it for the awards, eh?"

"I'd rather have nothing to polish and keep my head on my neck."

"You and me both."

The cameramen wandered off.

Megan wrapped her arms around herself. Her ribs ached, her knees were weak and her eyes brimmed with tears.

"Hey, hey, ignore them. It's just gossip, nothing else. James is fine." Brendon gripped her elbows. "He's fine, I just know it."

"But you *can't* know that," Megan said, blinking back tears. It was no good, one from each eye rolled down her cheeks. "And I haven't been able to get in touch with him for weeks now. Not a word. Each day, hour, minute that goes past makes me feel further away from him and all the more frightened. What if he's been shot? Or what if he's dead in a ditch? Maybe he'll never be found. Perhaps he'll just never come back and be lost to the jungle and the drugs and those horrid men forever."

"Don't be ridiculous. Of course you'd know. Someone would get word to you if he was hurt."

"But we're not married yet, I'm not his next of kin. And I've never even met his family. Would they even think to tell me if the studio informed them something had happened to him?" She sat heavily and touched her wet cheeks. "I'm just some woman living in his house, worrying about him."

"That's nonsense, he'll have left word at the studio for them to let you know if…" He tutted. "I'm not even going to say it, this is rubbish talk. He's fine, he'll be home soon."

Megan stared at her best friend through misty eyes. If only she felt as sure as Brendon did – then perhaps she wouldn't have the sensation of falling into a black hole.

12

Brendon offered to go back to James' house with Megan and stay the night, but she knew he'd planned to meet up with Zane for a late dinner. So instead she sent him on his way to have a nice time—a trip to the uber-trendy Ballers was something he'd been looking forward to all week, and one of the reasons he'd been dressed so sharply. And the guy deserved to be spoilt and have fun.

She knew she hadn't been the greatest of company lately—between feeling like she'd been run over by a steamroller, hugging the toilet bowl and freaking out about the whereabouts and life status of her fiancé, she'd been as much fun as a wet blanket. It would do him good to have a break from her woes and worries, and besides, all she wanted to do was curl up and let the weariness consume her tired bones. All the way home she'd been fantasising about getting out of her clothes and off her feet.

At least, and for this she was thankful, she'd been able to facilitate Brendon's first television appearance. She'd bet good money he'd be on some kind of show again in the near future. He'd seemed to naturally know how to work the camera and had been so at ease and comfortable in front of it. When they'd gone off script a little, he'd been witty and funny and his sunny personality had shone bright for all to see. Any producer worth their salt would spot that and snatch him up for a similar programme. With a bit of luck, he too would be getting a prominent profile in LA as a fashion pundit in no time at all.

Brendon's dinner at Ballers, she knew, would consist of him excitedly regaling Zane with every last detail. She just hoped Zane would be as enthused about it for Brendon as she was. She was sure he would be—the pair were getting on fabulously and she'd never seen Brendon so settled or besotted. He'd flitted from one short-term relationship to the next in London, but here in LA, it appeared he'd found the person he'd been searching for.

Perhaps there'd be wedding bells in Brendon's future, too. That was a thought that made her feel warm inside. To see him settled for the long term would be wonderful.

After alighting from the cab, Megan let herself in to the beach house. She turned off the alarm then switched on the overhead light in the main room. She spent a moment fiddling with the dimmer switch and kept the room in semi-darkness. Having spent a few hours under the glare of the studio lights, it was a treat to be in the shadows.

Out of habit, she glanced at the landline answer machine, hoping to see that little red light flashing. He'd said he'd use that phone if he couldn't get through on her mobile, so it had become a beacon of hope.

But there was nothing. No message—as usual. It was hard to ignore the weight of worry that draped over her like a cloak and was even heavier with each passing hour she had no contact with James. Though what could she do other than wait and hope?

Hope, now there was a thing. It was a thread she had hold of—a thin, delicate thread that could snap at any moment.

Kicking away her shoes, she headed for the bedroom, enjoying the cool floor on the soles of her feet. She peeled off her dress then tossed her underwear aside. The en suite reminded her of James every time she stepped into it. Memories of sharing the shower with him filled her mind as she flicked on the tap.

If only he was here now to wash my hair and hold me close. If only he was here now to…

But he wasn't, and that was something she was living with.

She washed, rinsed and dried. After using sweetly scented body lotion she longed for comfortable clothes, soft cotton pyjamas that were unrestrictive and slid against her skin.

Would she have this hypersensitive sensation for the whole pregnancy or was it just this first few weeks? Perhaps she should grab a copy of that book Brendon said he'd been reading – *Get Clued Up When You Get Knocked Up*. She'd have a look on Amazon next time she was online.

As she thought of Brendon, her phone beeped. She picked it up. It was a text from him.

Be strong. Hope is not gurgling its last breath. James will be home to you and the bambino before you know it. Love you my little sweetpea XXX

She smiled and sent him a few happy faces in reply, and at the same time her stomach rumbled. She was hungry. It had been hours since she'd last eaten, but as she padded into the kitchen she was unsure what to eat or even what she fancied.

She stared into the fridge and studied a pot of red pepper hummus, a bland vegetable broth Brendon had made, and a pack of fancy-looking sushi. Nothing appealed. She picked up a big carrot. After scraping it, she munched on the moist vegetable the way a rabbit might and enjoyed the fresh flavour coating her tongue.

Despite doing her best to feel relaxed, the overheard conversation between the cameramen had rattled her nerves. Her chest was tight and her shoulders had knots in them. She had no idea if she'd get any sleep with all the unanswered questions rattling around her brain.

Heading to the balcony, she then opened the door. The breeze was stronger now and the curtain bloated then flicked into the room, just tapping the side of the sofa. After stepping outside and pulling the door to, she reached for the thick blanket James kept in a wicker basket full of beach towels beside the outdoor shower.

The ocean roared, its continuous, predictable boom a strange comfort when everything else seemed at odds in her life. Wrapping the huge tartan blanket around her shoulders and folding the ends over her legs, she then settled on a soft lounger and stared at the black ocean through the glass screen that lined the balcony. The white tips of the waves glowed in the moonlight and the dark shadows of the depths made her wonder just what lurked there.

She finished the carrot and tucked her hands beneath the blanket, curling her fists into the material to hold it close. At least now she knew she wasn't the only one who'd thought James and Grant were nuts to be going off on their crazy adventure to El Salvador. It seemed that Grant's friends, fellow cameramen, were of the same opinion. The idea was beyond perilous, more than dangerous…it was a trip for risk-takers.

If only James were home now and it was all over. What she wouldn't give to have him walk through the door and tell her it was all okay, and he wasn't going back. That he was home now, to be a family with her and their baby.

She found herself resting her hand over her belly. Would their child be a daredevil, an adrenaline junkie, or be happy to live in imagination the way she'd done most of her childhood, with a head full of stories and pictures?

Despite her fears for James, she was smiling. She already loved their tiny baby. Its soul was part of hers and would always be in her heart. She had a longing to meet him or her, to study the face she suddenly yearned to see, check all fingers and toes were in order, and breathe in the scent of her child's hair.

An image of James cradling a tiny child swaddled in a white blanket, his eyes damp with emotion and his big hands gentle, besieged her.

She closed her eyes, the picture settling her nerves and soothing her. It would all be okay, it had to be. How could they have a child and it not work out?

She tugged the blanket up to her chin as a ripple of tiredness came over her. It beckoned her thoughts to a dreamy place and tempted her with reveries of the future. Would they stay living here and have a beach baby, a toddler who was at one with the nature along the oceanfront—cherubic face, curly hair, bucket and spade in hand?

Before long she was drifting asleep. She didn't fight it.

Her bespoke bridal shoes. Winter Shoes. There was something wrong with them. She was in a cold, dark church again. Walking down the aisle. But this time there was no one else there. Instead of facing all those disapproving guests and an angry Dylan, the pews were deserted, as was the altar.

Nothing.

No one.

Not even a vicar.

Her dress was big, hot and cumbersome. Her shoe heels were loose and her feet slopped around in them as if they were many sizes too big. It was hard to walk but she was reluctant to sit in the dim light, for an eerie feeling had spread over her. As though she was being watched, or followed. All was not as it seemed. Menace lurked in every corner.

Turning on the spot, the dress swelling, she hunted for her mother, her father, her sister Olivia. They weren't there. She called out for Georgie, Brendon and Zane over and over, until her throat was sore.

Where were they all? How could they leave her?

James. Where was James? She needed him. It was a real soul-deep ache for him to be somewhere in the depths of the church, waiting for her. She craved his arms around her, his body next to hers and the sound of his voice whispering reassurance, that it would always be okay if they were together.

A beautiful, bright, golden light shone through the arched doorway. She headed for it, instinctively knowing there was safety in the sunshine. She had to get out of the church. It was full of demons and ghosts of times gone by. Fears and pain and things she'd left behind which had no right to be rearing their heads again.

She broke into a fast run but was hindered by the enormous dress and the loose shoes. Despite her efforts, puffing and panting, working hard, she was getting nowhere. It was like running through treacle, trying to sprint with limbs made from lead.

Suddenly she fell, the air being knocked from her lungs. Crying out, she gripped her ankles, fearing they were both broken. But instead she found her broken shoes, the heels snapped off, the straps torn in two with frayed ends.

But it was the soles that upset her the most. The glitter had fallen off. All around, like a sea of tiny diamonds, the glitter winked up at her. Frantically she tried to press it onto the shoes, tapping, rubbing, smoothing it over the soles. Her heart was beating wildly, her eyes foggy with tears. Why wouldn't the glitter stick? Why wasn't it working? What was happening?

Where is James?

"James," she called. "Help, I need you. Where are you?"

It was so important to get the sparkling dust in place. For some reason she felt sure it would fix everything if she could only get that to stay on her soles the way it was meant to. All would be right with the world. She'd be able to stop running.

The bells were ringing. Clattering in a rhythmic chime. Ding. Ding. Ding. Ding.

She looked around, seeking help. There must be bell ringers.

Nothing. The dark, deserted church wasn't offering her support or sanctuary – it was hindering her, pulling her under. Allowing her fears to stab at her conscience over and over.

The bells were getting louder. Louder still.

Megan opened her eyes and stared at the gently undulating ocean. Breathing fast, she touched her chest and willed her heart rate to settle.

That had been a horrible church dream. One she hadn't had for a while now. Not since the disaster that had been her non-wedding to Dylan.

But still the ringing noise continued. Tinkling from the house.

"The telephone!" She threw the blanket aside and jumped up. A woozy rush hit her but she ignored it and dashed into the living room and grabbed the phone.

"James?" she gasped.

"Megan. It's me."

"Oh, thank God. James, I've been so worried." Her body felt heavy. Her knees gave way and she sat on the floor with her legs crumpled beneath her and the phone squashed to her ear. "Are you okay?"

"Yes, I'm fine. What about you?" His voice sounded remote and quiet.

"I can only just hear you. This line isn't very good." She nipped her thumb and index finger over the bridge of her nose and closed her eyes.

Please don't let us get cut off.

"I'm sorry," James said. "I've had to pay a restaurant owner in Tecoluca to use his phone. I haven't got long."

"I'm glad you did—pay, that is. I really needed to hear your voice."

"And I yours. I miss you."

"I miss you too, desperately." She paused. *Should I tell him about the baby?* The words were on the tip of her tongue. But something told her not to. She still wanted to see his face when she broke the news. Have him in front of her so she could hold him afterwards.

But what if he never comes back?

What if he never knows that he has a child?

She shook her head, banishing the terrible uninvited thoughts. "I was on the Lavinia show for a second time."

"You were. How did it go?" he asked.

"It was great. We were let down by the other guest who was supposed to be hosting with me, so Brendon stepped in at the last minute."

James chuckled. "And I bet he was in his element."

"Oh yes, he was brilliant, a complete natural. I'm sure he'll get more work like that."

"Good to hear."

"Plus it was nice to have him at my side, not nearly so nerve-racking to host a show when one of your best mates has your back."

"Always good to have your mates around when things push your comfort zone."

He paused and Megan wondered what he'd done that had been pushing his comfort zone.

"How is filming going?" she asked, even though a thousand other questions were running through her mind.

"Okay. We've got some great footage, real exclusive stuff in awesome remote locations."

"Is it…dangerous? I mean, is it as bad as you thought it would be?"

"Let's just say we're glad to have a couple of very capable security guys in tow. But no, it's not too bad. We've been sensible with our plans and our movements. There are definite no-go areas and we haven't ventured into them."

There was something about his tone that made her think he was placating her, making it out to be more of an easy ride than it actually was. And as for no-go areas…as far as she was concerned the whole country was a no-go area.

"I've tried to call several times," she said. "It usually goes straight to voicemail. Though it did ring once, for ages. I thought you might answer that time." She thought back to London and sitting in the restroom with Brendon and Georgie. "It must have been an odd moment when you had a signal."

"I know, I heard it, but would you believe I couldn't pick up."

"Oh, I see." She paused. "Why not?" That somehow hurt more than if the call simply hadn't connected. She bit on her bottom lip.

He chuckled. "We were navigating a rope bridge that spanned a gushing river, it was a two-hand job, gripping on. I couldn't let go even for a moment or I'd risk falling."

"That sounds horrible." She suppressed a shudder. A rope bridge, hundreds of feet up, rocks and water beneath—that was the stuff of nightmares, and she knew she didn't need any more fodder for them. Thinking about the guns and drugs was enough for her imagination.

"And when I got to the other side my phone ran out of battery," he said. "And the jungle isn't exactly rife with charging points and our portable one died in the humidity."

"I suppose." She stood, moved to the sofa, then sat with her feet tucked up. "So where are you heading to next, from Tecoluca?"

"We've managed to secure an interview with a farmer about five miles from here. He's a friend of one of the guys we got chatting to in this bar last night, which is why we're back here. The gangs have been stealing from him and beating him and his family for years, so he's prepared to speak out."

"Wow, that's amazing, but…what if these gangs get wind of the interview once it's broadcast, won't they hurt him more?"

"We'll hide his face, disguise his voice. He'll be anonymous."

"Oh yes, good idea."

"And then, once that's done, I think we'll call it a wrap and head home."

"What? Really?" *Have I just heard him right? He's coming home?*

He chuckled. "Yes, really. We have several hours of footage, and with this last crucial interview, we'll be able to produce not just a quality documentary but unequivocal evidence of what's going on here. The world will have to take notice."

"That's great. That you're coming back to LA, and the footage, too, of course, but mainly…mainly I just want you to come home safe and sound."

"I will soon."

"Do you know when?"

"Three days, four at the most."

"I'm so relieved. I can't wait to see you."

"It won't be long now. Listen, I have to go, the owner of this place is making weird hand gestures at me and he's a huge bloke with a gun in his back pocket."

"A gun."

"Don't be alarmed, everyone around here has one, and

remember I've got my two security guys with me, they've got my back."

"Of course, I understand." God, she hated guns. They just weren't part of her life, never had been and hopefully never would be. "I'll see you soon. I love you so much. Take care."

"I will, and I love you, too, Megan."

13

Megan slotted the phone back onto its stand. Her heart was beating wildly, her emotions spiralling. James was coming home. In just a few short days he would walk through the front door and she'd be able to hold him, kiss him, tell him the news.

She wrapped her arms around herself. Relief combined with impatience—the moment that he was at her side again couldn't come soon enough.

A glance at the clock told her it was well past midnight. She wondered if Georgie was awake and did a quick calculation of what the time was in the UK. Yes. Chances were she'd be up. She was back from her honeymoon now and would be getting ready for work.

After wandering into the study, she flipped on her laptop and hit Georgie's number on FaceTime.

Within seconds Georgie was there, smiling and sipping a cup of tea. "Hey, bestie, how is it going?"

"I'm good, Mrs Ellis, how about you?"

"Wishing I was still on honeymoon, but there you go, life can't be one long holiday, can it?"

"Be nice if it was." Megan reached behind herself, found one of James' sweaters and shrugged into it.

"What time is it there?" Georgie asked. "You're up late."

"I know. I couldn't sleep, then I had nightmares—"

"Not the church and shoes and devils' hands clawing at you from the aisle again?"

Megan shuddered. "Yes, that sort of thing. It was the glitter, though, this time. I couldn't get it to stick to the soles."

"You have the oddest anxiety dreams," Georgie said. "Most people have their teeth falling out, or they find themselves in the middle of a shopping centre stark naked, but you, it's all about churches and shoes."

"It was a traumatic experience, the whole jilting Dylan thing."

"Yes, but it's in the past now. Ancient history."

"You're right, I know you are."

Georgie frowned. "You didn't hear from him again, did you? While he was in California."

"No, not a peep. He must have done what he'd said he was going to and taken in the sights, headed to Las Vegas."

"And he'll be back in the UK by now, won't he." She rolled her eyes. "I hope I don't bump into him in Tesco."

"Ah, he's okay. He's over it now, moving on." Megan shrugged. "Thank goodness."

"Hey, wasn't it your night hosting the *Lavinia Heats It Up Show?*" Georgie slapped the palm of her hand against her forehead. "Shit. I'm so sorry, I did think of it but then totally forgot to text."

"It's okay, the time difference is a constant battle."

"So how did it go?"

"Amazing?" Megan grinned. "Not least because Nina Charles let us down at the last minute and the producer, Larry, offered Brendon the chance to take her spot."

"No freakin' way!" Georgie clapped her hands over her cheeks, her eyes widened and her mouth hung open. "You are kidding me?"

"Nope. He came on, looking pretty dapper too in a Ted Baker paisley shirt, and absolutely nailed it. He was a natural and the audience loved him."

"Well of course they did, what's not to love?" Georgie shook her head. "This is incredible, you two are flying high in LA, totally rockin' that place. I bet they don't know what's hit them." She giggled. "So when does the Megan and Brendon Show kick off?"

"Oh dear, he's already mentioned that." Megan laughed. "He's got grand ideas that he's no doubt plotting with Zane right now."

"Are they still going strong?"
"Yes, very. They're at Ballers tonight, living it up."
"Ooh la la, very posh."
"We'll go, next time you're over."
"I'd like that, a lot."
"And you'll have to bring your new husband."
"Definitely, he's desperate to get over and see all the sights. He's sick of me going on about it."
"Plan it whenever you can, there is plenty of space now that I'm living here, at James'."
"Yes, I suppose. Brendon's rattling around the rented house alone, is he?"
"Well, he's either here or at Zane's apartment at the moment. So the place in Venice Beach is sitting empty a lot of the time. We'll have to decide whether to renew the rent next month."
"You don't need the place, do you, not now you're living with your fiancé." Georgie waggled her ring finger. "And talking of James, have you had chance to tell him the baby news yet?"
Megan shook her head. "No."
"Wow, really?"
"I've only spoken to him once, just now, and it didn't seem right to tell him on the phone."
"But you were going to here, in London, at my wedding."
"I know, but it was different then somehow. The information was so new to me. But now that I've had a chance to get used to the idea, absorb the fact that in a matter of months I'll be a mother, I want to tell him face to face. See his reaction, you know?"
"Yes, I do know. I think I'd be the same with Tom. I'd want to look into his eyes, see his smile, then have him hold me afterwards."
"Exactly." Megan paused. "Are you and Tom going to try for a baby soon? You always said you wanted a big family."
"Well, as you mention it..."
"What?" Megan had a rush of excitement. *Is Georgie*

pregnant, too? Have they made a honeymoon baby? "Are you?"

Georgie laughed. "No, no. But I didn't bother renewing my pill prescription this month, so who knows, perhaps soon, by the end of the summer, I'll have a bun in the oven, too."

Megan laughed. "That would be so amazing. We can go baby clothes shopping together."

"And plan nursery colour schemes together." Georgie grinned.

"Yes."

"And talking of nursery, are you going to be using that room, the one you're in now, as a nursery?" She gestured around the neat, wood-panelled study Megan was sitting in.

"I hadn't really thought about it." Megan studied the huge rainforest picture that she knew James loved and his hefty shelves that were stuffed full of books. He had a wall dedicated to DVDs and a massive filing cabinet that he was always dipping in and out of when chatting on the phone. "The trouble is," she said, "he uses this room all the time. Where would all of this stuff go?"

"Is there another room you could use?"

"Well yes, there's a guest room, it's got a double bed in it but not much else. It has a big window, floor to ceiling, that faces out towards the ocean."

"That sounds perfect. Can you imagine how soothing it would be for a baby to listen to the waves?"

"Yes, you're right." Megan pictured the room in her head. It was painted off-white, the window was recessed, ideal for a rocking chair that she could use to sit and hold her baby when soothing him or her to sleep. It had a large walk-in wardrobe, currently containing a few of James' warmer clothes that he rarely wore in LA and a box of Ordnance Survey maps. It was home to a small stepladder and a basket holding a few token Christmas decorations that she couldn't ever imagine James bothering with if he were on his own.

"You should get started on it," Georgie said. "As a surprise for when he gets back."

"That's a great idea. I could just lead him in there instead of telling him straight out, and he could guess."

"I'd so love to be there to see his face if you did that."

Megan was on a roll. "I could get a cot and a mobile and a rocking chair and a changing table and—"

"Stop, stop," Georgie said then laughed. "Yes, all of that, you should do it, get Brendon to help you, but don't buy anything without taking a photograph and sending it to me. I want to feel like I'm there with you."

"You are. In here." Megan pressed her hand over her sternum. "I think about you all the time."

"And I think of you. But it's only a flight away, not that far really. In the olden days, it would have been a steam boat and horse and carriage across the Wild West. We have to be grateful for the modern times we live in."

"Yes, you're right."

"And still on the subject of James, have you any idea when he'll be back in LA to see this beautiful nursery?"

"Actually..." Megan's mood brightened. "Pretty soon, from what he's just told me."

"Really? That's great news." Georgie held up her hands. "And he's okay? What else did he say?"

"Yes, he's fine. In some place called Tecoluca. No idea where that is, other than it's not a popular holiday destination."

"No, that would be too easy a documentary to make. One about holiday destinations." She rolled her eyes.

"Would be a lot less scary though," Megan added. "But on the plus side, he said only another three or four days and they'll be getting on a plane back to LA. One more big interview to do, apparently, that will consolidate the rest of their footage."

"That is a relief. I had visions of him being out there until after the baby was born."

"Oh, don't." Megan pulled a face. The thought of going

through it all without him was horrendous. She had her first scan coming up, and attending that alone had been playing on her mind. Now, if James was true to his word and there were no hitches, he might even be able to go with her.

"But it's all fine." Georgie smiled. "This time next week you'll have forgotten he was even away."

"I hope so."

"Have you spoken to your mother?" Georgie asked.

"No, not yet. I was going to FaceTime her in a minute actually. I didn't think I'd be able to hold it together before."

"What do you mean?"

"Telling her about the baby when I hadn't heard from James for so long. One sympathetic word from her and I'd be mush and on a plane to Sydney."

"I know what you mean. But you've heard from him now."

"Yes, so I'll be able tell her she's going to be a grandmother without becoming an emotional wreck."

"Good for you." Georgie glanced at her watch. "Listen, I've got to run. When you speak to your parents, can you say thank you to them for the lovely wedding card and present? I've popped thank yous in the post, but you know, it really was very sweet of them."

"They think the world of you and Tom, you know that."

"And I think the world of them. Bye for now, try and get some sleep tonight."

"I will. Catch you soon."

Georgie disappeared and Megan pulled in a deep breath. This was it—the moment had come to tell her parents that they were going to have another addition to their family. She hit call and listened to the tinny sound rattling through the speakers.

Within a few seconds, her mother's face appeared. She was smiling, her hair was piled on top of her head and she wore a summer T-shirt. "Hi, Megan, what a lovely surprise."

"Hi, Mum."

"Is everything okay, dear?"

"Yes, fine."

"Is your handsome fiancé all right? Have you heard from him?" She looked worried.

"Yes, this evening in fact. His filming is going well, nearly finished, so he'll be home within days."

"That is a relief, we've been so worried about him." She pressed her hands together as though sending a quick thankful prayer heavenwards.

"And what about you all?" Megan asked. "Everything ticking along uneventfully?"

"Yes, we're all good. Your dad has been out playing golf all day, Olivia got an A in English and Maths tests at school and I've been into the city with Melody."

"Sounds fun, did you buy anything nice?"

"No, just lunch and then window shopping really. I'm lucky I have plenty of clothes, and I've long since stopped buying anything for Olivia. I always get it wrong." She tutted. "Just like I did for you at that age."

"Teenagers are pretty picky about what they wear."

"You can say that again."

"But on that subject..." Megan said, touching her belly with the flat of her palm. Her mother couldn't see her make the gesture, but it felt instinctual to hold herself that way. "There will be someone you can buy little outfits for soon."

Her mother tipped her head and narrowed her eyes.

Megan could almost see the cogs of her mind working.

"What do you mean?" she asked quietly.

"It wasn't planned, and it's sooner than maybe we would have had it happen but..." Megan paused. "Mum, I'm so happy it has happened, it feels so right, what I've always wanted and I love James so very much."

"Oh..." Her mother clasped her hand over her mouth. "Are you?"

"Yes. I'm pregnant."

"Megan." Instantly her eyes filled with tears. "If you're

pleased then so am I, you'll make a wonderful mother, you really will. And I know just how well suited you and James are so why wait?" She twisted in her chair. "Derek, come here, Megan has news, big news."

"I will be big soon." Megan laughed. "Very."

"I was your age when I had you. It's a lovely time in your life to become a mother."

Megan spotted her father coming into view. "Hi, Dad."

"Hey, darling, how are you? And why aren't you asleep?"

"I couldn't tonight, but I will soon."

"She's pregnant. Our baby is going to have a baby." Megan's mother tugged at her husband's sleeve.

He sat on the spare chair with a bump, his mouth hanging open.

A wave of nerves washed through Megan.

"Is it true?" he asked.

"Yes, James and I are starting a family."

"Wow."

Megan was worried—he'd gone a little pale.

"So soon after the Dylan fiasco," he said. "And we haven't even met James in the flesh yet."

"Don't be ridiculous, Derek," Megan's mother said. "Dylan and Megan were never right for each other and it's clear James is her soul mate, so why wait? They're getting married, for goodness' sake."

"Yes, I know and I'm thrilled." He smiled. "Really I am, but something has to be done."

"What?" Megan asked nervously. "What has to be done?"

"We're coming out there, as soon as possible, within the month. I'll look at flights as soon as this call ends."

"Really?" Megan could hardly believe what she was hearing. She'd see her parents so soon. It was like a wonderful dream to think that might happen. "And Olivia, too?"

"Yes, Olivia, too—her exams are coming to an end, so it won't hurt for her to have some fun time with her big sister in LA."

"Dad, Mum, you know I'd adore that, and you can stay at the Venice Beach place. Georgie and I were just saying that there is plenty of room there for visitors."

"Then it's a plan. I'll get your mum to text you the dates."

"I'm so happy. Really I am. I thought it would be ages till we all got together again."

"Darling, if I'm going to be a grandfather, I want to have a beer with your future husband and make sure everything is in order."

"You've chatted to him on FaceTime," Megan said.

"Yes, but that's not the same. We're coming over." He glanced at his watch. "I'll leave you to your mother, I'm going to pour a beer now, wet the baby's head."

"You do that after it's born," Megan said with a giggle.

"Practice makes perfect." He blew Megan a kiss. "Rest up. See you soon."

"I will, Dad." She turned to her mother, who adjusted the screen so she filled it again.

"I think he's quite emotional really, Megan."

"Do you?"

"Yes, he's always said he'd relish being a doting grandfather."

"We'll have to make sure we have lots of trips to spend time together."

"Of course we will." She appeared thoughtful for a moment. "As long as James is okay with that."

"Sure he will be."

"Good." She smiled. "And what did he say when you told him about the baby?"

"Er…"

"Megan!" She shook her head. "Don't tell me he doesn't know…"

"How could I tell him? I only found out myself a short while ago and he's been away. I didn't want to break the news on the phone. I've had no choice but to wait until he comes back."

"I suppose." She paused. "Funny how history repeats

itself."

"What do you mean?"

"I was over three months pregnant before I told your Dad about you."

"You were?"

"Yes, he'd been away on business, in Malaysia. I had the same emotions as you're having right now—it had to be heard directly from my mouth—so I understand why you're delaying telling James, totally."

"And Dad was okay that you hadn't mentioned it?"

"More than okay, I think he was relieved that he hadn't had to cope with that information when we were apart. When there's news that big, news that binds two people for all of time, it has to be said face to face. You've done the right thing, my darling. You really have."

14

James

James swiped his machete through a tangle of vines, slashing them in half and further clearing the way forward. The trail through this part of the jungle was tough going, worse than they'd thought it would be. Already they'd narrowly missed walking into an electric fence, and earlier, in the distance, Brent had spotted a lookout post staffed by a man with a machine gun. It had taken them an extra hour and a half to navigate around him through the thick undergrowth.

Now sweat dripped from James' temples, his black shirt was stuck to his back and a blister on his right foot hurt with each step.

But he wouldn't and couldn't give up now. They were so near. The farmer who'd agreed to talk to him was only a few kilometres away. And once he had this interview, this final piece of footage, he'd be able to head home.

A huge bug landed on his shoulder—bright green, with bulging eyes and two-inch feelers—and he batted it away. Ahead of him Grant paused, took a slug of water, then continued. He too was dripping with sweat, his shirt damp and his hair clinging to his nape. He had the extra burden of all the filming equipment but he would rarely accept help with it. It was his job, he said, to lug it around.

"We should veer west in a few minutes," Luca said, studying his compass. "And that will take us to the Valle el Potrero and your man."

"How much longer, do you think?" Grant asked.

"Another couple of hours." Luca looked between Grant and James. "You need to stop?"

"Nah, keep going," James said. "Sooner it's done, sooner we can start making our way the hell out of here."

"Roger that, boss," Luca said. He turned and continued to lead the way.

Behind him, James was aware of Brent pushing forwards. They'd all reached the same jungle-weary state. The heat, the humidity and the constant need to be on high alert had got old. Plus, ever since he'd spoken to Megan the evening before, he'd had a steady ache in his heart that he knew would be there until he was holding her in his arms. It was as if a piece of him were missing when they weren't together. The first few days here, weeks even, he'd been so focused on the job, adjusting to his environment, that missing her had only come over him in waves every so often, stealing his breath and making his chest feel tight. Now it was a continuous longing. He craved seeing her smile. He wanted to sleep with her curled up next to him and wake with her limbs tangled with his.

She was the one. He had no doubt about it. The person he wanted to start and end his days with for the rest of his life.

And if she really hated him doing this kind of thing as much as she said she did, then maybe it was time to skip some of the wilder adventures he set himself up for. Adrenaline rushes, perhaps, weren't all they were cut out to be.

"Stop." Luca held up his hand.

The rest of the group halted.

James peered through the vegetation. A large spider with red spots hung from a web, but he barely saw that. What he did notice was a group of men and a military-style Land Rover sitting in a clearing. They were some distance away, down a slope, but it was still too close for comfort.

"Militia," Brent muttered. "Likely the exact ones we're trying to avoid."

"Fuck," Grant said quietly. "Now what?"

"We can get round them, if we make no noise." Luca indicated a route where the undergrowth had thinned, beyond which there appeared to be a rocky outcrop covered in tangled ribbon-like vegetation.

"At least we know where they are," James said, trying to ignore the rapid beating of his heart. The men he was looking at were heavily armed and didn't appear as if they'd think twice about using their weapons. He didn't fancy making their acquaintance any time soon.

"Come on," Luca said, flicking his hand to the right. "And for Christ's sake, don't make a sound."

James tucked in behind Grant and they slowly and carefully headed out of the immediate vicinity of the militia. James had understood why the farmers were reluctant to talk, but seeing it for real, what they were up against, made it all the more important that they kept the anonymity of the man they were meeting safe.

Thankfully they reached the valley they were searching for without further incident. As with many of the hidden farms they'd visited, the cocoa crop grew tall and healthy and swayed innocently in the breeze.

Brent checked a small satellite device. "We're exactly on the co-ordinates we were given."

"Mmm, I don't see any signs of life." James shielded his eyes from the sun and glanced around. "Do you?"

"What's that, over there?" Grant pointed over Luca's shoulder.

They all turned to look.

"It's a person," James said, "walking this way."

Brent put his binoculars to his eyes. "I'd bet good money this is your guy."

"At last." James adjusted his backpack, then sloshed some water into his mouth, not caring that it ran down his chin to his chest. He headed off to meet the man they knew only as Mateo, running his fingers over the cocoa crop as he stomped ahead.

The farmer stopped.

So did James. He held up one hand. "Mateo?"

"Si."

They continued to draw closer and came to meet at a wooden structure that had three sides and a roughly fashioned tin roof. A sooty pile of stones surrounded what had once been a fire and a tatty blanket sat in the darkest corner.

"It is good to meet you." James held out his hand.

The man took it and shook. His fingers were bent with arthritis, his skin was dark and scars circled his wrists as though he'd been bound with something tight.

"Hola," he said, showing that he had very few teeth.

Luca arrived at James' side. "I'll translate, as planned."

"Thanks," James said, indicating the shade of the shelter.

The man said something in rapid Spanish.

Luca responded.

"What did he say?" James asked.

"He's just confirming that his face won't be shown, that you won't use his real name."

"I don't know his real name. Did you reassure him?"

"Yes. He says he feels it his duty to expose the struggles of his people. That he is old and his life over, but his family must not have to live with his words that will be seen as traitorous by the gangs that rule them."

"Tell him I am very grateful for his words and that his bravery will be seen by many, many people worldwide who will all admire and respect what he is doing."

Luca spoke to Mateo again, who listened, his eyes wide, then nodded.

Grant pulled the camera from its protective covering.

Mateo backed up, holding his hands high. "No, no."

"It's okay," James said, "he's filming me asking the questions, not you. You won't be in the shots, I promise." He nodded at Luca.

Luca relayed the information. Mateo responded with an anxious nod.

"He's nervous," Luca said. "He wants to stand in the shadows so that he will not be visible at all."

"I think that's a great idea." James nodded and pointed to

the darkest section of the shelter. "And I'll stand here, in the sunshine, so that the camera won't be able to pick up any more than his outline if it pans that way."

Mateo, with more reassurance in Spanish from Luca, tucked himself into the shadows.

"You ready?" James asked Grant.

"All set."

James glanced at Brent. He was holding his gun and surveying the perimeter of the crop field. His eyes were narrowed and a muscle flexed in his stubble-coated cheek.

Brent was clearly uncomfortable. With an armed drug gang only minutes away if they used one of the few dirt tracks and their vehicle, they were playing with fire.

But James had to keep his cool. He had to let Brent do his job while he and Grant got the footage. He cleared his head and recalled the questions he wanted to ask.

"Go." Grant gave him the nod.

"For this man's safety," James said, looking at the camera, "he'll be known only as Farmer One. We will not be showing his face and his voice has been changed. There is good reason for this, because just by agreeing to speak to us, a foreign reporting team, his life would be in grave danger, as would that of his family.

"And it's taken great courage, great bravery for him to defy the drug gang that controls his land to speak out. But in this country of chronic political hostilities, out of control drug production and unimaginable violence that is an everyday occurrence, he feels it is time something was done. And if this man can stand up to show the world what is happening, surely it is time that the world stood up and took notice."

James turned to the darkened shed.

"Farmer One, tell us about the crops you grow now and how they differ from times gone by."

Luca translated.

Mateo replied, his voice quiet but firm.

Again Luca translated, giving James the response to his

question.

James moved on to his next question—this time about the gang that ruled the farmer's land.

Mateo replied with detail.

James was thrilled. He'd responded with great understanding of his people's struggle and his government's inactions.

The interview went on for about twenty minutes, James delving into all the particulars he wanted the world to hear.

"Let's go," Brent said, suddenly. "I can hear an engine, some way east of here. I'm not liking where we are right now, we're sitting ducks."

"I hear you, buddy," Grant said, lowering the camera.

"Thank you, Mateo, *gracias.*" James held out his hand.

Mateo took it and shook firmly, but his attention wasn't on James—he was staring into the undergrowth to the east. He too could hear the noise of the engine.

"We're moving," Luca said. "Now."

The unmistakeable sound of a vehicle rumbled towards them.

Mateo took off at a sprint, running at an incredible speed for an elderly man. Within seconds he'd disappeared into the darkness of the jungle.

"This way." Luca slammed his hand on James' shoulder. "Quickly."

They ran back the way they'd come. The clearing was uphill and the ground uneven, but James pounded onwards, desperate for the cover of the jungle, despite the fact that it had made his life so hard the last few weeks.

The Land Rover was close, its wheels snapping branches, its engine roaring.

Suddenly a shot rang out.

"Fuck!" Brent, who was ahead of James and Grant, spun around, his weapon ready. "They've spotted us."

Terror coursed through James' veins. How had they let this happen?

They bolted into the undergrowth.

Another shot rang out.

Brent fired back this time.

A string of shouts in Spanish. The car horn sounded in a crazy string of excited hoots.

"Now what?" James asked, glancing around. Running would be exhausting in the jungle. But they had to put distance between them and their pursuers.

An image of Megan popped into his mind's eye.

He had to get home. For her.

"This way," Luca said. "Hurry." He set off at a fast pace, weapon at the ready and following a trail.

James and Grant followed, Grant struggling with the camera, which he hadn't put away properly. James reached out and grabbed the heavy case that was banging awkwardly on his back. "I've got this."

"Thanks."

"Jesus Christ," Brent cursed. "Get a move on."

"We'll hide out at that outcrop we saw on the way," Luca said, darting forwards and ducking beneath the branch of a tree.

"How will that help?" Grant asked breathlessly.

"We'll lay low. They'll expect us to keep running."

"Fuck," James muttered. Hiding, lying low, that was their best bet? He didn't think the odds were great. The men chasing them likely knew this jungle like the backs of their hands.

But he had no choice but to go along with Luca's suggestion. He took heart in the fact that he knew Luca had been in plenty of similar scrapes over the years and was still around to tell the tale.

On and on they went. James leapt over branches. Leaves, vines and twigs scraped at his cheeks. His chest ached with the exertion, but he pounded on.

The gunfire had stopped, at least, but he knew that was because they were out of sight now, not because they'd got away from the gang. They'd be following on foot, determined to find the foreigners on their land. They wouldn't have to be geniuses to know that James' plan was to expose them to the world. One look at the footage on Grant's camera and that would be plain to see.

And then what?

Torture?

Ransom?

Shot?

None of that sounded appealing.

"This way," Luca said, swiftly detouring to the right.

James followed, wondering where he was being led. He'd lost his sense of direction.

Finally the outcrop, which was like a cliff edge with bulbous red-grey rocks, stood before them. It was practically hidden with rambling plant-life that lolled downwards in thick curtains. The leaves were emerald green and stroked the jungle floor.

"Get behind it," Luca said, parting the curtain of foliage. A huge black frog landed on his foot. He ignored it. "Hurry."

James did as he'd asked, moving behind the greenery so that his back was up against the cool rocks.

Grant pressed in beside him and they pulled the glossy leaves and rope-like branches close, hiding themselves behind them.

"Now stay still and be quiet—in fact, don't even fucking breathe," Brent said, also covering himself with foliage.

"Jesus," Grant muttered, his shoulder brushing James'. "How the hell did it come to this?"

James didn't answer. A stab of guilt went through him. This whole trip had always been his idea.

James would never forgive himself if anything happened to Grant.

Brent and Luca were hidden, too, either side of James and Grant, likely with their guns trained on the trail they'd just run. For what must have been the hundredth time, James was thankful that he'd paid for such sharp professionals. If they hadn't had these two guys with them, they really would be up shit creek without a paddle.

He tried to slow his breathing and peered through a tiny gap in the leaves. He couldn't see anything so instead he listened for the gang – there was no car noise, no shouts. It was eerily quiet.

He wondered if he preferred it loud and frantic. At least then he knew where they were.

Suddenly he spotted movement.

Grant tensed.

James figured he'd seen it, too.

Two men, dressed in camouflage gear and wearing black caps, came into view. One had a cigarette between his teeth. Both were holding large guns and scanned the forest floor as though checking for tracks.

James sent a quick prayer heavenward that they wouldn't be able to see where they'd gone.

The men stopped and began to talk in Spanish. James had no idea what was being said but tried to make sense of their hand gestures and body language. He deduced that one wanted to keep going forward and the other was making an argument for going back to the vehicle.

Something tickled his neck, just below his right ear.

He froze.

A dry, slithering sensation set every nerve in his body tingling and his scalp tightened.

He strained his eyes to see.

Snake.

A lime green snake with a flat, triangular head and prominent nostrils was sliding over his shoulder, its forked tongue poking in and out, tasting the air.

James gritted his teeth. The urge to yell, flick it off, was almost overwhelming. But if he did he'd draw attention and get them all shot.

He glanced at Grant, fear gripping him. He had no idea what kind of snake it was.

Grant was looking his way. He'd seen the snake and his eyes were wide. He gave an almost imperceptible shake of his head.

James knew he couldn't react. The snake, even if deadly, was the least of his problems right now.

He clenched his fists and shut his eyes.

Megan.

If he died she'd be all alone. She'd have been right to worry about him coming to El Salvador and her greatest fears would come true.

He couldn't do that to her.

He had to get out alive.

James opened his eyes again. The snake's head was at his elbow now. The creature was in no rush to be on its way. The men hunting them continued to debate.

He swallowed—fear tasted bitter—and remained very still, only just taking in air.

In a flash the situation changed. In the distance three shots were fired. The two militia took off back the way they'd come. Clearly, they'd been summoned to return to the vehicle.

James blew out a juddery breath, still not daring to move.

"Thank fuck for that," Luca said, appearing in front of him and parting the vegetation.

"Can you help me out with this?" James asked, gesturing to the snake.

"Sure." Luca reached up by James' neck and picked up the snake's tail. He held the creature aloft. "Wouldn't want a bite from one of these, it's a pit viper. Only a baby one, but still." He threw the snake into undergrowth to their right.

James stepped out of the greenery, his heart beating rapidly.

"Well done, mate," Grant said, clapping him on the shoulder. "Not sure if I could have kept my cool like you just did."

"Didn't have much choice." James wiped a drip of sweat from his brow.

"And we haven't got any choice but to get as far away from here as possible before sunset," Brent said, still surveying the vicinity, his weapon at the ready. "Let's get going."

15

Megan

"Thank you," Megan said to the deliveryman. "Just put it there please, that would be great."

He set the last box she'd ordered from Babies' Bedrooms down in the hallway of the beach house.

"A signature, ma'am." He held out a clipboard and pen.

"Of course." She signed, then after he'd left, she shut the door.

"Oh, this is so bloody exciting," Brendon said. "And for the record, I think it's utterly adorable that you're getting the nursery ready before James comes home. What a way to let him know he's going to be a daddy."

"We'll have to be quick with these finishing touches, though," Megan said. "When he called from San Salvador earlier he said his flight was at seven this evening and he should be home before midnight."

"That gives us oodles of time, it's only six." Brendon tore at the tape on the box. "Lord have mercy on the cuteness!" He held up a cushion embroidered with a pale yellow rabbit sitting in a meadow of pale grass and white flowers.

"Ah, that's for the rocking chair," Megan said, taking it. "Good, it's nice and soft, just as I'd hoped it would be. The base of the chair is padded but I needed something to rest my back on."

"Of course, we don't want Mummy to be uncomfortable." Brendon delved into the box again. "And a matching blanket. So adorable."

"There should be two pictures—watercolours—in there, too, the same style with little rabbits."

"Yes, here they are." He pulled two pictures in white

frames out and pushed aside the protective bubble wrap. "Do you want me to put them up?"

"Are you up for more DIY?" Megan asked with a giggle.

"Hey, I'm the DIY king…or queen, whichever way you look at it." He shrugged.

"It's just the cot…"

"I know, I know, I turned the air blue when I was assembling that, but it wasn't my fault, the instructions were all wrong." He paused. "And besides, we agreed to never mention it again."

"My lips are sealed." She did a zipper motion over her mouth.

"So, I'll get the hammer and some picture hooks from James' toolkit. You go and decide where you want these hanging."

Megan wandered into the guest bedroom that was now the nursery. She'd been lucky and managed to get a cot, changing table and rocking chair all delivered the day before and with the guest bed tucked to the side of the big room, she was pleased with how it was set out.

She just hoped James liked it. Other than the furniture and a couple of pictures, she hadn't done anything drastic to the room. She was aware it wasn't her house, despite James telling her to consider it home, so she hadn't wanted to make huge changes without consulting him. And besides, whatever happened, she'd be needing the new furniture in a few months anyway, so it had had to be bought regardless.

"On this wall?" Brendon asked, pointing to the exact spot Megan had planned for the pictures.

"Yes, that's perfect."

As he set about hammering in the two small hooks, Megan let out a sigh of relief. In just a matter of hours James would be home. Back where he belonged—at her side and not in some god-awful war zone where anything could happen.

She could hardly wait.

"There, what do you think?" Brendon asked, stepping back to admire his handiwork.

"Lovely," she said, setting the cushion and blanket on the rocking chair. "That pulls the whole thing together."

"Oh, oh, one more thing." Brendon dashed from the room. Within seconds he was back. "This too." He handed her a large bag with Babies' Bedrooms written on the front.

"Brendon, you shouldn't have, really, you've done so much already." She pressed her hand to her belly.

"I know, I know, but I'm going to be an uncle and I'm so excited. And when I saw this I couldn't resist."

Megan smiled and pulled out the gift. It was a mobile to go above the cot. It had tiny rabbits in pastel colours hanging from it and several bright orange carrots. "Thank you so much. It's lovely and it matches perfectly."

"Yes, I thought so." He took the mobile from her and set about attaching it to the white cot. "There, what do you think?"

"It's lovely. And I think we've done an amazing job in the few days we've had to get organised. This place is all ready for a new addition to the family."

"Well, let's face it, Hot Guy didn't exactly leave you with a shabby room to do up, did he? This place is stunning whatever is in it."

"It will have a baby in it soon."

"It will indeed, sweetpea." He set a quick kiss on her cheek and gave her hands a squeeze. "But now I have to run. So I'll leave you to your romantic reunion with your sexy, daredevil fiancé and catch up with you tomorrow. Those contracts have come through from Harrods—we need to get them signed and sent off."

"No problem, I'll call round after my dating scan."

"Ah, the scan, yes, that's tomorrow, isn't it? Make sure you get a picture of the little tadpole for Uncle Brendon to coo over and show everyone."

"Of course."

Megan spent the next few hours preparing for James'

homecoming. She lounged in the bath, treating herself to a hefty glug of a new foam that was designed for expectant mothers and smelt of powdery flowers. She slathered herself in cocoa butter—a must, apparently, for staving off the dreaded stretchmarks. Not that she even had a bump yet, but she figured she couldn't start that skin regimen too soon.

After pulling on a tight dress, then a pair of skinny jeans, neither of which felt right, she opted for soft cotton trousers and a crop top. The evening was warm and as usual the French doors were open, letting in the breeze. She piled her hair high and kept her makeup minimal. The only jewellery she wore was her engagement ring.

She headed into the kitchen and was aware that the usual nausea hadn't been nearly as persistent today. In fact, it had hardly been there at all after its initial onslaught when she'd woken up. Perhaps that unpleasantness was finally coming to an end. She'd be grateful if it was.

So with a glass of lime and soda on the go and humming a summer tune, Megan started preparing James' favourite meal. He adored Italian and in particular a fresh pasta, pesto, manchego cheese and cherry tomatoes dinner she'd made for him a few times. Her plan tonight was to get it all prepared and cook it when he arrived home. It would only take a few minutes and would be delicious served up hot.

Once organised, Megan set the table. She took extra care and used a fresh white tablecloth, the best glasses and placed a red candle in the centre. She even found some white linen napkins in the drawer and folded them neatly on the table. By the time it was dark and the candle was lit, she figured it would give a lovely romantic ambience to their meal, a bit like their first date in London when he'd taken her to Bettino's.

She sighed at the memory. They'd had champagne, been fussed over by Rosseta and spent the whole evening talking about everything and nothing. Back then she hadn't been able to believe her luck that she'd met such a gorgeous, grounded, humble, incredible man, and now he was her fiancé and she was carrying his child.

Happiness was a warm, soft feeling that floated through her and now all she needed was to get him home.

Which wouldn't be long.

She glanced at the clock. Another hour, then he'd be coming through the door.

It was dark outside so she shut up one of the French doors, calming the wafting curtains, and sat on the indoor sofa staring out at the ocean.

As soon as she relaxed back on the squidgy cushions, tiredness washed over her. It had been a long, busy day, but fun too, and her excitement at seeing James had kept her going.

She reached for a spare cushion and propped it beneath her head, nestling into it. Perhaps she'd close her eyes, just for a few minutes.

Soon she was drifting into a relaxed state. Her thoughts became jumbled.

Images of the yellow rabbits and the cot filled her mind. She pictured her parents in the nursery with her, fussing over their new grandchild, and her sister Olivia sitting in the rocking chair cradling her tiny niece or nephew.

It was such a nice dream, a safe dream. She thought of Georgie with her, also holding a baby, her and Tom's baby, and how content they'd both be. Enjoying being mothers together.

And above the whole picture, smiling and warm, was James, his arms like a big, protective shield around them all.

"Hey, baby."

She murmured, her eyes heavy. James was speaking to her. In her dream.

"I'm home."

Not in her dream.

She opened her eyes, her lids reluctant to pull up. She blinked several times.

James was right in front of her, smiling and cupping her cheek. Her heart rate picked up. Excitement and relief pinged through her.

"I'm sorry, I'm a bit later than planned," he said.

"Oh my God. At last." She threw her arms around his shoulders, burying her face in his neck. "You're here, that's all that's important."

He squeezed her close and ran one hand over her hair and the other around her waist.

Emotions bubbled up in Megan's chest, but she kept them in check. He was home, finally. He'd survived. He'd made it back to her. "I've been so worried," she said, her lips moving against his skin. "I'm so glad it's over."

"Me too," he murmured then kissed her temple. "Me too."

She pulled back and held him at arm's-length. He had more stubble than she'd ever seen him with, and his hair was messy. The skin around his eyes was creased, as though the sun had carved lines into it, and she could tell that his cheeks were a little hollowed. "Are you really okay?"

"Nothing a few good meals won't fix." He grinned suddenly. "And the love of a good woman."

"You know I love you."

"And I love you, too, I never want to be away from you like that again…ever."

"Do you really mean that?"

He nodded, his face serious. "Yes. I'm not doing that again. I've decided."

"But what…? I mean, what changed your mind?"

"It got pretty dicey out there for a while." He shook his head as though ridding a memory from his thoughts. "And for a moment it could have gone one of two ways."

"What do you mean?" She hardly dared ask.

"A bullet or home." He glanced away.

Megan covered her mouth. She'd been right to be terrified. Right to be angry that he was risking himself.

"And I realised," he went on, facing her again, "that I can't do that now. I'm not free and single anymore. I have you. All I could think was if something happened to me you'd be alone. And I don't want that. I never want to hurt you or put you through pain, Megan. I want to be here, living my life with you, seeing you smile, starting and ending each day with you, growing old with you." He closed his eyes and pressed his lips together.

"Oh, James. It's been horrible without you, made a billion times worse because I was so worried and it was so hard to talk to you. But if you really need to continue making these documentaries then I'll understand. We'll get through it somehow."

"I don't." He opened his eyes and took her face in his hands. "I mean I do need to keep making documentaries and they're never going to be about rainbows and butterflies, that's not the sort of guy I am. But from now on, it's going to be considerably less hazardous subject matter."

"That makes me very happy."

"You make me very happy." He kissed her.

It was a deep, passionate kiss that spoke a thousand words. Their tongues tangled and she clung to him, never wanting to let him go. And she wouldn't, not without one hell of a fight.

He pulled back and gripped his T-shirt between his shoulder blades. In one smooth movement, he tugged it off and discarded it.

"James," she said, running her hands over his chest. His collarbones were a little more prominent than usual, his ribs slightly visible. "Are you...?"

"I'm fine. I told you." He kissed her again, then said, "But no more talking, let me show you how pleased I am to be home."

He gripped the base of her crop top and peeled it off, breaking the kiss only for a second.

Megan reached behind herself and unclipped her bra. She pushed up against him, loving the feel of flesh on flesh and how his chest hair scratched her nipples.

He groaned into her mouth and slipped his hands up her back, as if wanting to touch all of her at once but not knowing where to start.

She did the same to him, running her hands over his shoulders, up his spine, along his biceps, making sure he was all in one piece.

Soon he'd manoeuvred her so she was flat on the sofa and he hovered over her, his face doused in shadows.

"Time for these to come off," he said, tugging at her trousers.

She giggled and kicked them away. She liked his plan.

He removed her knickers, too, and she lay there with the breeze tickling her skin and watched him shuck out of his jeans.

"We spent last night in San Salvador, a niceish hotel," he said. "But all I wanted to do was jump on the first plane here, to you."

"You didn't get the first one?" She faked a pout.

"The second, the first was full." He grinned and moved over her again.

He kissed her breasts, up to her neck, and settled himself between her legs. "You make everything feel right," he said. "There's so much crap out there in the world but you, you're perfect." Very gently, he eased inside her.

"James..." Megan gasped, curling her legs around his thighs. "Oh yes."

He stared into her eyes as he entered her fully, not blinking, not wavering, as though seeing into her soul.

Megan cupped his face in her hands, his bristly jawline scratching her palms. It felt so good, so incredible to be at one with him. And damn, the man was beautiful. Even in this haggard, tired state, he was more than perfect.

He began to move, rocking in and out.

Soon her breaths were coming quicker, the pleasure building. Her pelvis was heating, the need for release becoming more urgent. She tensed her abdomen, clung to him tighter. "Oh, don't stop, more..."

He gave it, quickening the pace and rubbing over her just how she needed it.

Bliss spiralled within her. Ecstasy spread over her skin,

contracting her muscles and stealing her breath.

James found his release, too, never breaking eye contact with her. He gritted his teeth and a full body tremble attacked him.

He stilled, panting, and brushed a few loose strands of hair from her cheek. "Nice welcome home."

"I'm glad you approve." She reached up and kissed him.

He twisted to the side and pulled her close.

"And I have dinner prepared for you, too."

"Mmm, what is it?"

"Your favourite, Italian."

"You're so good to me."

"You deserve it." She reached for his hand and kissed his palm. "Shall I go and make it now?"

"No, not yet." He tugged her nearer, slotting her neatly into alignment with his body. "Stay snuggled on the sofa with me for a few minutes. I've only just got you back in my arms, I'm not ready to part with you just yet."

She laughed. "It's only to go to the kitchen."

"I don't care. I want you here, with me."

Megan smiled and twined her fingers with his. She had no problem staying locked in his arms for a while. Then, once they'd had dinner, she'd take him into the nursery and get him caught up on all that had been going on while he'd been away.

She could hardly wait.

16

Megan's plan didn't quite pan out. They slept on the sofa for several hours, waking not to have dinner, but just to move into the bedroom. Within minutes they were both fast asleep again, wrapped in each other's arms, and didn't stir until morning.

And as she blinked open her eyes to the brightness of the daylight streaming in, Megan couldn't remember starting a day more perfectly, or, more to the point, without the nausea attacking her.

James was good for her, that much was evident. He made her world stable.

She stirred and, as she did so, James opened his eyes.

"Morning, gorgeous," he said, smiling.

She set a kiss on his shoulder and ran her foot down his leg. "I need tea."

"I'll go and make it," he said sleepily.

"No, you won't, stay there. You need pampering, Mr Carter, after what you've been through. I'll make you breakfast in bed as you missed out on your special welcome home dinner last night."

He grinned and stretched his arms above his head, twisting his torso so that the sheet tugged around his waist. "I'm not going to argue with that," he said. "And damn, I'd forgotten how good it is to sleep in my own bed, with you."

"And I'd forgotten how nice it is to have you here, in our bed." She smiled and stood, covering her nakedness with a silky black robe.

"Do you have to wear that?" he said, waggling his eyes and grinning.

"While I'm making breakfast, yes." She rubbed her hand over her belly. "I don't want to get splashed when cooking your bacon."

"Oh, bacon, you have no idea how good that sounds."

She tied a bow on the robe at her waist, and thought of their tiny baby growing in her womb. Soon she would tell him, after breakfast, then she'd show him the nursery and her secret would be out. James would know about the child they'd made.

After opening one of the French doors to let the morning sea breeze into the bedroom, she headed for the kitchen.

The neatly set table greeted her and she smiled. They'd been hungry for each other last night, not food, but that was okay—they'd enjoy the meal for lunch or dinner.

She flicked on the kettle and put teabags in the pot then set about making bacon sandwiches. It was the first time in ages she'd actually felt hungry, as if she would eat breakfast and keep it down.

So with the radio playing a happy tune, she whistled as she created breakfast. She laid a tray with napkins, cut big doorstops of white bread for the bacon to go between—James' favourite way to eat his morning butty—and poured milk into a pretty little jug that had seashells on it.

Walking back into the bedroom, she was dismayed and thought he'd gone back to sleep. She wanted him to enjoy his breakfast warm. But he must have heard her, because he opened his eyes then scooted up the bed, resting his back on the headboard.

"Wow, this is five-star treatment," he said, examining the tray Megan set before him.

"Are you hungry?"

"Starving." He smiled. "I made you a breakfast tray like this once, you know? It even had a flower on it."

"Did you?" Megan frowned, trying to remember.

"Yes, but when I took it up to the bedroom you'd gone."

"Ahh, yes, that."

"Mmm, that." He pretended to scowl. "You took quite a bit of chasing after, Megan Winter."

"Well, I wouldn't like to be an easy catch."

He laughed. "You certainly couldn't be accused of that."

She smiled and passed him his cup of tea.

He took a sip then set it aside and bit into his sandwich. When he'd swallowed, he said, "So tell me everything. What have you been up to? You hardly told me anything about the *Lavinia Heats It Up Show* on the phone and that sounded like amazing exposure. Plus…" He hesitated. "I'll confess I was a bit distracted. I really only wanted to hear your voice then hurry up and get out of there."

Again Megan thought of her big news. Possibly the biggest news ever. She had to force herself not to blurt the words out.

I'm pregnant. You're going to be a daddy.

"The show went really well. The producer was thrilled. And what was even better was the other guest let us down."

"And that's good?" He appeared confused. "Because…?"

"Because it gave Brendon a break. Larry, that's the producer, saw what a fashion worshipper he is, and let him come on with me. We had a great time. I almost forgot the camera and the audience were there, we were just chatting about clothes and shoes the way we normally do."

"Hey, that's great." He shook his head. "You never fail to amaze me, how you just take all this TV stuff in your stride."

She shrugged. "It's fun. Wasn't particularly planned but if it's good for Winter Shoes and people want to hear my opinion on things, then I'm happy to do it."

"I'll have to watch it," he said. "Is it on record?"

"Yes, you know Brendon, he likes to watch these things over and over."

James chuckled. "I do. I'll watch it later today, this afternoon."

Again Megan bit her back her words. That afternoon they'd be at the hospital, and she'd be having a scan. But she couldn't tell him that, not just yet.

But soon she would.

Soon she'd tell him it all.

She set aside the last of her sandwich and sipped her tea. She was impatient for James to finish his breakfast but she'd made him double what she'd had.

He made murmuring, approving noises as he ate.

Finally, his plate contained only a few crumbs.

"If being married to you means I get bacon butties in bed then I'm going to be a very happy man." He smiled and set a kiss on her lips.

"Is that all I'm good for?"

"You know damn well it's not." He drew her closer and wound his arms around her waist. "You are good for many things."

She giggled and pressed her hands on his chest. "Wait, there's something I need to show you."

"Can't it wait?" He kissed over her cheek to her neck, his stubble scratching her chin.

She squirmed, wanting his kisses but out of patience. It was time to tell him.

Wriggling some more, she freed herself from his embrace and stood, adjusting her now askew robe. "Come with me?"

He raised his eyebrows. "I had planned on staying in bed, for the morning, with you."

"We can still do that, but…"

"But what?" He raised his eyebrows and she knew she'd piqued his curiosity. "Megan?"

"Just come with me." She pushed her hair behind her ears. A sudden wave of nerves washed through her.

She'd been dreaming of this moment. Picturing how it would go in her head for weeks and weeks. And now it was here, that moment. She hoped, with all her heart, he'd be happy, that it would be the icing on the cake for him, too, the way it was for her.

He stood and pulled on a pair of black boxers. "What have you done?" He laughed but she sensed a hint of apprehension there.

"I haven't done anything." She smiled and took his hand. "It's what *we've* done."

"You're talking in riddles."

"So come on and I'll solve the puzzle for you." She tugged his hand and led him from the bedroom, across the living area and to the second bedroom that was now the pretty nursery.

"Go inside," she said.

He hooked his finger beneath her chin and stared down at her. "You like to keep me on my toes," he said. "I'm always guessing when you're around"

"Keeps life interesting." She swept her lips over his. "But just remember how much I love you, and how happy I am, here with you."

He didn't speak but she could see the love in his eyes, and some of her nerves calmed. With a love as strong as theirs, bonding them together, how could it not all be okay?

"Open the door. Go in," she said, stepping back.

He pulled in a deep breath and released the handle. Slowly he opened the door. It creaked slightly

He walked in.

She stared at the back of his head and knotted her fingers beneath her chin.

Silence.

She glanced at the cot, the rabbit pictures, the rocking chair and the changing mat. All exactly as she'd left them. Each cushion and blanket and tiny detail fussed over until she was happy with it.

He pushed his hand through his hair then turned to her.

His mouth was parted, his eyes wide. Several strands of his hair were sticking up wildly.

"We need this room to be a nursery," she said.

"A nursery," he repeated, saying the word slowly as if testing out the feel of it on his tongue. "A nursery for a baby?"

"Yes." She nodded and ran her hand over her belly.

His gaze followed her movements.

"I'm pregnant, James. We're going to have a baby."

"You're pregnant. But..." He shook his head slightly.

"Don't you dare say how." She laughed, but it sounded strained even to her own ears.

"Well no, I can guess how, but…bloody hell." Suddenly he dropped to his knees. He placed his hands on her hips and stared at her belly.

She brushed her hands through his hair, loving the feel of it between her fingers.

He reached for the bow on her robe and tugged it free. The material parted.

Leaning forwards, he placed a delicate kiss on her lower belly. It was such a gentle touch, as soft as butterfly wings brushing against her.

"James," she whispered.

He looked up at her, his eyes misted with emotion. "You've just made me the happiest man alive," he said, his voice tight.

She smiled as relief washed through her. "You're happy?"

"More than happy." He stood and pulled her close. "A baby, we're going to have a baby?"

"Yes, a family of our own."

He cupped her cheek and gazed into her eyes. "Just when I thought life couldn't get any better. It just has."

He kissed her—a deep soul-connecting kiss that seemed to fill her up with his love.

She never wanted to be apart from him again. This was where he belonged, with her and their baby.

A few hours later, Megan and James were navigating the corridors of LA's finest obstetric clinic.

He had a tight hold of her hand and she wondered if the news had sunk in for him. It had taken her a few days to get used to the idea and the baby was inside her.

"I'm so glad you came home in time for the scan," she said as they waited to book in at the reception desk. "I didn't want to come to it on my own."

"You wouldn't have. Brendon would have come with

you."

"And everyone would think he was the dad and we had some weird arrangement going on."

James looked slightly confused.

"He's the gayest gay bloke around. No one would believe we were…" She flicked her hand between herself and James. "A couple."

"True." He kissed her temple. "And for the record, I wouldn't want to miss this for the world. Had I known, I'd have run back from San Salvador the other night."

"You'd probably still be running." She giggled.

"True. Plane was the most efficient way."

"Next," the receptionist said with a smile.

"Hello." James stepped up to the counter. "Megan Winter for a scan with…" He turned to Megan.

"With Dr Sonny," she said.

"Is he good?" James asked, frowning.

"Came very highly recommended," Megan said.

"By who? Maybe we should—"

"It's just a scan," Megan said. "Relax."

"I can assure you Dr Sonny is the best of the best," the receptionist said. "You are all in very safe hands."

"See," Megan said with a smile. "It's fine."

James nodded and glanced around.

"And you can go straight through, he's waiting for you." The receptionist indicated a room to the left.

"Straight in," James said.

"Yes, come on." Megan tugged his hand then paused. "You okay?"

He nodded. "I'm fine. Really I am."

"I know it's all happened fast for you. I've had a while to get used to the idea."

"It has, but it's good, it's all good." He swept a kiss over her lips. "Come on, we shouldn't keep the doctor waiting."

They went into the room and were greeted by a man, possibly in his sixties, who wore large black-rimmed glasses. "Hello, Ms Winter, it's lovely to meet you." He held out his hand.

"Hello, Dr Sonny," Megan said, taking it. "This is my fiancé, James Carter."

"Pleasure to meet you," he said, then shut the door. "Do take a seat."

Megan looked around the room. It was set out like an office and had a nice view over the city, but in one corner was a surgical couch and a scanner on a chrome table.

For a moment she felt a little scared.

"Sit down, baby," James said, pressing the small of her back. "It's all okay."

She nodded and beat down a wave of nerves.

"I've just read your notes," Dr Sonny said, sitting behind his desk. "And it all seems very straightforward. No family history issues, no existing medical conditions."

"No, nothing like that."

"Anything in your family history, James, that might be genetic and I need to know about?"

James thought for a moment. "No, nothing that I can think of."

"Perfect." Dr Sonny stood. "We should get on with the scan then, make sure there is only one little baby in there."

"Twins?" Megan said, looking at James. "Why would there be twins?"

"None in my family," he said, also appearing alarmed.

"Not always familial," Dr Sonny said. "But I do find mentioning twins speeds this process up, gets the mums on the couch a little quicker."

And he'd been right—Megan was already sliding onto the cool leather and swinging her legs up. No longer worried about the scan, she was more concerned with how many babies she was carrying. Twins hadn't crossed her mind.

Dr Sonny switched the machine on and a screen lit up with a pale green hue.

James stood on her other side and held her hand.

"How has the morning sickness been?" Dr Sonny asked.

"Not great, but I've coped okay with it."

"And did you lose weight?"

"A little, perhaps. I didn't seem to fancy anything."

"Are you still feeling sick?" James asked, studying her with concern.

"Not really. I think you missed the worst."

"I'm sorry, I should have been there to bring you ice chips and mop your brow."

She smiled and squeezed his hand. "It's okay, Brendon soon got the hang of that."

He bit on his bottom lip and she knew he was berating himself for going away. But he couldn't have known—neither could she—when he'd gone to El Salvador.

"I need you to pull up your top and push down your pants, both just a little," Dr Sonny said, holding up a microphone-sized scanner that was coated in clear gel.

Megan did as he'd asked.

"This is a bit cold," he said.

She tried not to jump as the cool gel made contact with her warm skin.

James drew her hand to his mouth and kissed her knuckles.

Dr Sonny pushed his glasses up the bridge of his nose as he peered at the screen.

Megan tried to make sense of the strange shapes and the shadows and light areas.

"Ah yes," he said. "There we go."

"Is it okay?" James asked, leaning forward and frowning at the confusing image.

"Well, there is only one baby in there, you'll be pleased to know." He glanced at them both. "Unless you were hoping for twins."

"No, one is good," Megan said, then had to hold in a giggle so as not to move too much.

The doctor smiled and turned back to the screen. "This is your baby," he said, pointing out a blob in the centre. "The head, spine and legs, can you see? The knees are bent."

"Oh yes," Megan said. "Wow, I really can."

"That's amazing." James blew out a long, slow breath.

"And, it's the right size for your dates," Dr Sonny said. "Obviously later scans are much more detailed, but for now, everything is in order."

"That's such a relief," James said, squeezing Megan's hand. "To know that."

"Yes," Megan said, nodding. "It is."

"Would you like a printout?" Dr Sonny stared at them over the rim of his glasses.

"Yes please." She turned to James. "Brendon would never forgive me if I didn't."

James laughed, a little louder than usual. She guessed he was as relieved as her to know that everything was progressing as it should with their child. "Perhaps we could have two, Dr Sonny."

"Not a problem."

There was a whirring sound from a printer on the other side of the room.

"I'll just measure you." Dr Sonny wiped away the worst of the gel. He then took a tape from his pocket and conducted a couple of measurements over Megan's belly. "Well within normal parameters."

"Good," James said. "Really good."

"And that's us done." Dr Sonny popped the tape away. "And unless there are any problems, I'll see you in due course." He handed Megan a strip of blue tissue. "You can clean up the last of that gel and cover up."

"Thank you." She took it and wiped her belly. "And yes, we'll see you again soon."

Dr Sonny smiled and left the room.

James watched her wiping the gel away and straightening her clothes.

When she'd finished, she gave him a quizzical look. "What?"

"It's just..." he said. "I woke up this morning, so happy to be back in LA, with you, I didn't think I needed anything else in life, and now...now I realise I did, and it's this, our child. I've never been happier and it's you, Megan, who's made me this way."

Megan sat and wrapped her arms around his neck. "I'm glad. I'm happy, too."

"And…?" He frowned a little.

"What?"

"We should get married. Soon."

"Well, we are engaged."

"Yes, but I don't want to wait. I don't like us having different names when we check you in here. We should be married. What's wrong with today? Let's get married today. We can go find a registry office."

"Really? You can do that in LA?"

"I don't know." His frown deepened. "We'll drive to Vegas. It's only a couple of hours away. Find one of those little white chapels and have Elvis marry us."

Megan laughed at his serious face. "James, we can't do that."

"We can do anything we want." He cupped her cheeks. "And I want to be able to call you my wife soon, the sooner the better. We've made a child—that child needs his or her parents to be married." He paused and shrugged. "Call me old-fashioned, but that's just the way I feel."

"I like that you're old-fashioned." She paused. "And I feel the same, about getting married quickly."

He raised his eyebrows. "So we'll drive to Vegas, today?"

"No." She batted his arm. "My parents would hit the roof, and Olivia and Georgie and Brendon would have my guts for garters. They've been to one non-wedding of mine. If I have a real one, they'll want to be there."

James said nothing, but she could tell he was thinking things though, wondering how he could persuade her.

"How about," she said, "we make a date for two weeks' time. My parents are planning on coming out within the month anyway. Plus that will give me chance to speak to Georgie and Tom, get flights and book somewhere nice for a meal afterwards."

"It doesn't need to be a big fancy affair. As long as the day ends with you as my wife, that's all that matters."

"I know, I get that." She shrugged. "But I want a bit of the fancy stuff. I am a girl, after all. And besides, don't you think your family might want to come? Your mum and your sisters and Roxy?"

He paused then nodded. "Mmm, okay. Two weeks, but not a day over."

"It won't be. I promise."

17

Megan stood at the arrivals gate at LAX, scanning the doorway as passengers flooded into the United States.

The information board told her that the Qantas flight from Sydney had arrived fifteen minutes ago and she was impatient for her mother, father and sister to disembark and grab their luggage.

James laughed and gave her a hug. "Can't you keep still? It can't be good for you to be hopping about."

"I can't help it. I'm so excited. I haven't seen them for what feels like forever."

"So what's a few more minutes?"

"They seem the worst somehow, these last few minutes."

He kissed the tip of her nose. "Relax, it won't be long now."

Megan leaned into him and tried to calm the jittery feeling in her chest and stomach.

"Megan!"

Megan was suddenly tugged from James' embrace and pulled into a tight hug. "Wow, Olivia, I didn't see you come through the gate." Megan laughed.

"You were canoodling." Olivia hugged her tighter. "And I ran…fast."

"It's so good to see you." Megan's eyes stung. She'd known she wouldn't be able to hold back tears. "I'm so glad you're here."

Olivia held her at arm's length and looked her up and down.

"You've grown," Megan said.

"You haven't." Olivia frowned. "I thought you'd have a bump by now."

"Well, maybe there is a little one." Megan rubbed over the

tiniest swelling in her lower belly, barely noticeable even if it was being searched for.

"Megan, sweetie."

"Mum." Megan squealed, reaching for her mother, who was now at her side. "You're here."

They cuddled and rocked and laughed.

Megan suddenly felt beyond excited about the wedding that was planned for the next day. She'd been getting things organised with Brendon—and Georgie and Tom, who'd arrived two days previously—but now that her parents were here the celebrations could really begin. Now she could be excited.

"Dad," she said, tears pouring down her face.

"Darling." He pulled her into a tight bear hug. "How are you?"

"I'm fine, Dad, really I'm fine." She tried to hold back a sob but failed.

"So stop crying," he said with a laugh, though his eyes were misty, too.

"I can't help it, I'm so happy you're all finally here."

"And are you going to introduce us properly to your husband-to-be?" he said.

"Yes, yes, of course. Dad, Mum, Olivia, this is James."

"James," her mum said, reaching for him. "I know we've chatted plenty on FaceTime, but it really is good to finally see you in the flesh."

James gave her a chaste kiss on the cheek. "You too, Mrs Winter."

"Oh, stop that." She batted his arm. "I told you, call me Iris. Mrs Winter makes me feel so old."

"Okay, Iris."

"Nice to meet you, son," Megan's dad said, holding out his hand.

"You too, sir."

"I guess just Derek will do."

They smiled at each other. Megan knew they'd get on like a house on fire. Unlike Dylan, James would have no trouble keeping up with her father's conversations about current issues, and if he made the effort to take her dad for a round of golf, they'd be friends for life.

"Hi, James," Olivia said, biting her bottom lip and seemingly a little shy.

"Very pleased to meet you," James said, taking her hand and bowing low.

Olivia giggled.

"We should get going," Megan said. "We booked Blu and Brendon, Zane, Georgie and Tom are meeting us there."

Her father pointed at their suitcases. "But—"

"They'll be okay in the restaurant," he said. "If you're happy with that."

"Good plan. And I'm starving," Iris said. "I really can't cope with eating and flying." She pulled a face.

"Come on, then," Megan said, linking arms with her sister and mother. "Let's go and eat, I'm starving, too."

A couple of hours later, Megan looked around the table. It occurred to her that everyone she loved was in one place. *How often does that happen in a person's life?*

She sipped a glass of sparkling water and watched as James chatted to Olivia about her recent exams. Brendon was poking fun at Georgie while Tom sat back and watched—Georgie was holding her own. And her father had captured Zane in a conversation about where to find the best golf courses in Southern California.

"Are you feeling okay?" her mother asked, putting her hand on Megan's arm.

"I'm fine. More than fine. This is wonderful, to have you all here in LA."

"And when are James' family arriving?"

"His sister and niece live nearby, so we'll see them tomorrow. And his mother and other sister arrived yesterday and we all went out for dinner. They were going to join us for lunch but his mother struggled with the jet lag so we'll see them in the morning."

"I'm excited about that."

"Me too. My new mother-in-law is lovely."

"Well." Iris pulled a face and leaned close so only Megan could hear her. "I shouldn't say it, but she can't be any worse than Dylan's mother."

Megan giggled into her palm. "Yes, you're right. She drove me crazy with all that meddling before the wedding."

"And there's no time for meddling, is there? Not with it being so close now."

"I know, it's nuts, isn't it? Tomorrow I'll be a married woman." She paused. "And it feels so right this time. Last time, with Dylan, on the lead up to the big day I felt as though I was just going through the motions. It was something that was happening around me rather than to me. I lost sight of the fact it was a ceremony to bind me to Dylan, forever."

"Thank goodness you came to your senses." She touched her lips. "Oh, I really shouldn't have had that glass of wine, I can't stop myself saying what I think."

Megan laughed again. "It's fine, it's the truth. And if I hadn't…well, we wouldn't all be here now, would we?" She glanced at James. "And I wouldn't be marrying the love of my life."

Her mother smiled. "That's true." She took a sip of water. "So, the dress. I know hardly anything about it. Tell me all."

"Actually." Megan glanced at her phone to check the time. "I need to go and collect it. It needed an alteration on the neck line, it was a bit tight." She indicated her generous cleavage. "But it will be ready now. Shall we go and do that, just me and you, and James will drive Dad and Olivia to the beach house so you can all see the sunset."

"I think that sounds like a wonderful plan." She gave Megan a quick hug. "I can't wait to see it, the house and the dress."

"Zane," Megan said, waving to catch his attention. "We're going to head to the shop, to get my dress."

"Yes, do go, darling. I got a text about an hour ago saying it was in and ready for collection." He paused. "Are you sure you don't want me to bring it in the morning?"

"I think I'll sleep better if I have it beside me." Megan smiled. "Thanks, though."

"You okay to do that, or shall I drive to Rodeo Drive and get it?" James asked as she stood.

"No, no, it's fine." She rested her hand on his shoulder. "Mum and I will enjoy the trip. I'll see you in an hour or so, at home."

"Okay." He reached for her hand and kissed her palm. "Go carefully."

They headed into the bright sunshine and hailed a cab. Megan was pleased the sickness had completely gone. When she'd been at her worst, being in a car had been torture.

"So," her mother said, "how are the other plans coming along?"

"All organised. But you know what Brendon's like. Give him an event to plan and he's in his element."

She chuckled. "He's the best."

"He really is. I don't know what I'd have done without him while James was away. He's a laugh a minute most of the time, but when you need him to be solid and serious, he really is."

"And Georgie?"

Megan sighed. "I miss her so much. I'll never not miss her if James and I make LA our permanent home."

"And do you think you will?"

"Yes. No reason not to. His work is here. Winter Shoes can be run from here and London. Enid is a gem in the UK office. And there's more in the pipeline for me on the *Lavinia Heats It Up Show.*"

"Really? That's great."

"It was fun." Megan placed her hand on her belly. "But if it all slows down for a while, if Brendon can take more control for the next year, that's cool, too. I've got a baby to concentrate on."

Her mother nodded.

"Not to say I don't want to work afterwards, I do. It's just I don't want to be torn between career and baby. I want it to be a happy medium."

"It will be, darling, you've always managed to do that. And James is going to be a wonderful, supportive father, I can tell."

"He's great, isn't he?"

"He really is quite a catch." She smiled.

"Oh, here we are. This is LA Hype. Zane is the manager here. This is where my first shoe launch was, on my birthday."

"I remember you telling me. And this is where your dress is?"

"Yes. Zane insisted on one particular seamstress to alter it." She rolled her eyes. "He wouldn't let anyone else near it."

They stepped out of the cab. Megan paid the fare, then they wandered into the quiet shop.

The air conditioning swept over them. A new hat collection occupied the centre stand where Megan's shoes had once taken pride of place. She didn't mind too much. Her autumn collection was scheduled to inhabit that spot again soon.

"Hi," Megan said to an assistant she'd seen several times before.

"Hello, Ms Winter, have you come for the dress?"

"Yes."

"Zane just called, said you had to try it on before you left the shop in case there was any problem."

"Really?" Megan shook her head and smiled.

The girl shrugged. "Just passing on what my boss said."

"Oh, Megan, don't keep me in suspense anymore, go and put the dress on." Her mother clasped her hands beneath her chin. Her eyes were wide. "I'm desperate to see it."

"All right." Megan laughed. "I will. But just so you know,

it's nothing like the last one."

"Good."

The assistant indicated to the right, where a plush curtain separated the changing room from the main shop. "It's just in there, waiting for you."

"Thank you." Megan went in and drew the curtain. Not that there were any other customers in the shop. Rodeo Drive was like that. The small boutiques were so exclusive that few people could afford to shop there, but when they did, they spent big bucks.

She smiled and pushed the clear plastic protection away from her dress. The moment she'd seen it she'd known it was the one, even though it wasn't an official bridal gown.

Zane and Brendon had ooh'ed and ahh'ed so much that it was actually the only dress she'd tried on. It had felt so right for a beach wedding.

A beach wedding.

Another tumble of excitement rolled through her. Getting married where James had proposed—with soft sand underfoot, by the rolling waves of the Pacific, and the Californian sun above—was the perfect solution to finding a venue last minute.

Quickly, she stripped out of her summery skirt and top, then carefully stepped into her dress.

She tugged it up. The silky lining was cool and soft and as she fastened the zip she saw that the alteration had made it the perfect fit.

Smoothing the material over her hips, she admired her reflection. She hoped James would like it. If he was expecting a meringue, a Disney princess dress, he wasn't getting it. This one was off the shoulder, made entirely of white lace and although it was fitted, it was also a little loose. She liked the fact that it was short, too. Her legs were tanned and she was planning on going barefoot onto the beach—even she couldn't walk in sand wearing heels.

"Are you in it yet?" her mother called through the curtain.

"Yes, open up."

The curtain was pulled back and her mother stood there staring with wide eyes. "Oh, Megan, it's perfect."

"Do you like it?"

"It's beautiful, just like you, and it's so…"

"What?"

"It's simple, it's not trying to be anything it's not. A bit like you and James."

"What do you mean?"

"Well, you love each other, that's all you need. You don't have to have all the fancy extras, though my goodness I'm sure he could afford it."

"That's true, as long as we have each other, we're happy." She paused. "And the baby now, of course."

"Yes, the baby." Her mother pressed her lips together.

Megan studied her. "What is it?"

"I shouldn't say, not yet."

"Shouldn't say what?"

"We've made a decision, your dad and I. Well, it was more of an opportunity really and it's come at the perfect time and…"

"Tell me." Megan held out her hands. "Don't say you're moving back to the UK just as I'm making the decision to stay out here."

"No, no…actually we're moving here, to California."

"You're what?" Megan couldn't believe she was hearing right. Not in her wildest dreams had she ever thought her parents would move to the US. "But…how…? Why?"

"You know your dad has been doing some consultancy work? Well, they want him in San Diego, for the next few years at least. And Olivia has finished her exams now, we've been investigating colleges over here for her, but she's thinking of taking a gap year and, well, it just makes sense."

"Mum…really? Is this all true?" Happiness pinged around inside Megan. Her knees were a little weak.

"Yes, yes, it's true. We're going to be based about an hour out of LA. It's meant to be, and now with the baby and everything…" Her words became shaky. "How could we not say yes?"

"Oh, I'm so happy. This makes everything perfect." Megan flapped her hand in front of her face. She didn't want to cry but tears were coming.

"I know. I want so much to be a proper grandmother. Not just one who sees her grandchildren twice a year on a visit. I want to be there for you now, while you are pregnant, when the baby is tiny, then I want him or her to have memories of me as they grow up. And your father, he's already planning which golf courses he can take his grandchild to."

Megan held in a hysterical giggle. "Likely be swinging a golf club before he or she can walk."

"Yes." Her mother pulled her into a hug. "I don't want to crease your dress but…"

"I don't care. The dress will survive. This is the best news ever. I can't tell you how happy I am. It's the icing on the cake."

"And do you think you'll be able to act surprised when your father tells you tomorrow?"

"No. No. I really don't." Megan laughed again. "I'm just too happy. I can't stop smiling."

18

Megan slipped out of the dress and back into her own clothes. It was as though her world had gone from being thrown into the air when James had been away and she'd first found out she was pregnant, to now all slotting neatly into place.

Her mother was chatting to the attendant in LA Hype about a new range of handbags just in, but stopped and smiled when Megan appeared.

"I have these, just as well we didn't forget." She held up a stunning pair of Winter bridal shoes that had gladiator-style straps and diamanté details. Naturally the soles were glittery, the way all Winter Shoes were.

Megan had designed them some months previously and when she'd picked out her dress, she'd known they'd go with it beautifully. She might be planning to be barefoot on the beach, but back up at the house she wanted heels—high sparkly heels.

"Thanks, Mum. Brendon said they'd been delivered here." She smiled and set the shoes in their box. "I've been looking forward to wearing these."

"Do you have flowers ordered?"

"Of course, do you think Brendon and Georgie would let me forget?" Megan laughed.

"True."

"I've opted for orchids. They're coming tomorrow."

"Oh, how lovely. And the cake?"

"Also coming tomorrow." She smiled her goodbye to the shop assistant and linked arms with her mother. "The caterers are bringing it, along with the rest of the mountain of food James has organised."

"And what's the cake like?"

They pushed outside into the lingering heat of the day. The scent of the sun on the road and buildings lay heavy in the air and a yellow Lamborghini purred past.

"It's quite simple, white, with more orchids and the icing resembles lace, like my dress. It's not too big."

"I don't suppose it needs to be."

"No, there's only a few of us."

"And are you okay with that? I mean, when it was Dylan the church was…" Her words trailed off.

"Packed. I know. Everyone we knew had been invited, or so it seemed. It was too much."

"It certainly seemed that way when you ran back up the aisle and out the door."

"Not my proudest moment."

"I was proud of you, for listening to your heart even though you knew the consequences would be hard to face, for a while at least."

"Thanks, that means a lot."

Megan hailed a cab and it drew up at the kerbside. She opened the door for her mother and gave her home address to the driver.

"But this time when I get married," she said, sliding into the back, "I feel like it's the people I really want there. James feels the same way, too. There's only a handful of friends I want to share my special day with, and family of course. So why have the masses fill a church? When it was Dylan and me, I'd imagine they were sat in the pews having bets on how long we'd last. How many years until the divorce lawyers were called in."

"Oh, I don't think so." Her mother frowned. "People wouldn't be so cruel."

"Mum, come on. Looking back, I can see how mismatched we were. He wanted to change me. I wanted to please him, make him happy, but equally I'm not prepared to change for a man. I might have put up with it for a while, until my eyes opened and I saw our marriage for what it was, but I couldn't have lived like that forever. It would have erupted at some point down the line and likely got really ugly."

Her mother took her hand and squeezed it. "I feel much more content, in my heart, when I see you with James. I understand that I don't know him very well, and I hope that changes soon, but the way you smile when you talk about him. The way he looks at you when you don't even know you're being watched by him. It's love. There's no two ways about it."

Megan squeezed her mother's hand back. "It is love. And do you know what?"

"What?"

"I love being in love."

"Good, because from where I'm sitting, you two are a match made in heaven."

Back at the beach house, Megan took great delight in showing her parents and Olivia around her new home, including the huge decked balcony that tomorrow would play host to their reception.

"You're so lucky," Olivia said, sighing as she looked at the sky that was now turning into a wash of flame red as the sun drooped towards the horizon. "I'd love to live here. This house is amazing."

"It is a bit special." She glanced at James. It was mainly special because he was there. If he'd only had a shed in downtown LA, she'd have thought it equally lovely.

Well, maybe not quite.

"You'll be able to spend lots of time here, when you're living in California," Megan whispered into Olivia's ear.

Olivia turned to her, her expression one of shock, which quickly turned to delight. "Mum told you?"

"Yes. But I have to act surprised when Dad tells me." She giggled.

Olivia giggled, too. "I'm so excited. It's going to be awesome. And I'm going to be an auntie and a California girl. I can't wait."

Megan wrapped her sister in her arms.

"Everything okay?" James asked, heading onto the deck with a beer.

"Yes, fine." Megan nodded enthusiastically. She'd tell him later that their child was going to have one set of grandparents living nearby. Not only that, they'd have their support too as they set off on this journey as parents.

He took a slug of beer and studied her.

He'd guessed something was going on. He knew her too well. But Megan didn't mind. In fact, she liked that.

"We're going to make a move now, Megan," Georgie said, also coming onto the decking area. "Need my beauty sleep for the big day."

"You're already beautiful," Tom said, kissing her cheek and wrapping his arm around her waist.

"Uh, these two just need to get a room," Brendon said, rolling his eyes as he stepped outside. "Anyone would think they were still on honeymoon."

"Well, it wasn't that long ago," Georgie said. "And anyway, you can't talk. I just saw Zane whispering in your ear, and by the way you grinned, it was something absolutely filthy."

Brendon coughed as a rise of colour hit his cheeks. "Was not." He raised his phone to his ear. "I'll call the cab."

"Can you make it two cabs?" Olivia said. "We'll head back to our hotel now. Dad was snoozing on the sofa when I saw him ten minutes ago. Jet lag is a bummer."

Brendon nodded then spoke into the phone, organising transport for everyone.

Within minutes, Megan and James had said goodbye to their guests and had the house to themselves.

"Did you enjoy your afternoon with your mum?" James asked.

"Yes, I loved spending time with her. It's been great to catch up with Georgie the last few days, but I really needed some one-on-one time with Mum."

"I'm sorry you miss her so much." He tucked a strand of

hair behind her ear.

"Well, the thing is..."

"What?"

"I won't have to miss her for much longer."

"What do you mean?"

"They're moving out here. Mum, Dad, Olivia. Down near San Diego."

"I don't understand?"

"Dad's job, he's been offered work in California and because of us, the baby, he's accepted."

"Really?"

"Yes. Really."

James grinned and wrapped his arms around her waist. "That's wonderful news."

"It is. I'm so excited."

"Why didn't they say anything to me, though?" Concern crossed his eyes.

"Apparently it's a secret, for now."

"Worst-kept secret ever." He laughed and his features softened.

"I know." She linked her hands behind his neck and brushed her lips over his. "I'm so happy. I was happy anyway, happier than I thought possible. But now, to know that they'll be around, only an hour or so away and not an ocean away, it's filled my heart with joy."

He smiled. "You fill my heart with joy."

She raised her eyebrows. "I'm pleased to hear it, Mr Carter. And our soppy talking reminds me, have you written your vows?"

"I have." He nodded seriously. "Have you?"

"Of course."

"Good, because tomorrow is only going to end one way."

"And how's that?"

"You'll be Mrs Carter and you'll be wearing a wedding band, one that I've put there."

"And so will you be—wearing a wedding band, that is."

"Yes. I'll be yours and you'll be mine. Forever." He swept

her up and held her to his chest.

"James." She giggled. "What are you doing?"

"Taking my bride-to-be to bed."

"For my beauty sleep."

"Something like that." He headed towards the bedroom.

Gently he laid Megan on the bed then turned on one of the low lights that sent a buttery glow over the room.

Megan watched as he peeled off his T-shirt and shucked his jeans. She knew she'd never get bored of looking at his athletic body. She adored the way his muscles rippled beneath the surface of his skin. How his shoulders were broad and his waist neat. His legs had a coating of dark hair and she loved how they felt when pressed against her smooth ones.

He climbed onto the bed next to her. "Are you planning on sleeping fully dressed?"

"You know I'm not." She smiled up at him then accepted the kiss he placed on her lips.

As he kissed her he undid her skirt and let it pool at her ankles. He then set to work on the buttons on her blouse.

Soon she was naked. His skin was warm to the touch and the scent of his fading cologne filled her nostrils.

"I want to make love to you," he whispered. "Tonight, tomorrow night, every night for the rest of our lives."

"Yes." A tremble of need tugged at her belly. "That's what I want, too."

He drifted his hand from her knee to her thigh. A flash of worry crossed his face.

"What is it?" she asked, cupping his cheek.

"The baby. Will it be okay if we…?"

"Of course."

"Are you sure? I mean, you always seem little and delicate anyway and now, with you being pregnant as well…"

"It's fine, honestly. I've read the books, there's no problem with me or the baby so we can carry on as usual with our bedroom activities."

"Bedroom activities?"

"That's the term they use in the book." She licked her lips, retrieving the lingering flavour of him.

"Ah, I see." He stroked up her leg again, higher this time. "Well, as long as you're sure."

"I'm sure. It was fine the other night, when you arrived home, and besides, do you really think we could go months without…?"

"No. Definitely not." He ducked his head and kissed his way down the column of her neck, over her throat and to her breasts, his stubble lightly scratching her skin.

Megan closed her eyes and slotted her hands into his hair. The way he caressed her, touched her, it made her feel so loved.

It also made her greedy for more.

He slipped lower down the bed, settling himself between her legs.

She arched her spine and tensed, knowing what was coming. And damn, he was so good at doing that.

He teased her for a moment, the anticipation of his hot mouth on her driving her insane with want. She writhed and squirmed and groaned.

Eventually he gave it to her.

She fisted the sheet and bit down on her lip. He was working her towards release, building it up.

She thrashed her head from side to side, longing for the ecstasy to race around her body.

Her pulse boomed in her ears, her belly tightened and her breath was hard to catch.

Suddenly it was there—a wonderful spilling point that bubbled over and sent bliss racing over her nerve endings, contracting her muscles.

"James. James. Oh, yes…" she cried, jabbing her heels into his back.

He stayed with her, easing out the pleasure, then kissed his way up her body.

She was still breathing hard. "Wow."

"Wow yourself."

She held his cheeks and kissed him.

He delved his tongue into her mouth in a slow, languid kiss. He seemed in no rush, happy to take his time.

Eventually her breathing came back to normal. She sighed, enjoying the sated sensation and the way her limbs were heavy.

"Sleep now," he said, stroking her hair.

"But? You…you haven't."

"It's okay. I wanted to give you pleasure. I'll save myself for our wedding night."

She looked at him quizzically. "It's a little late for those kinds of traditions, don't you think?"

"Maybe that's so, but by rights we shouldn't even be spending tonight together, if we were doing anything traditional, that is. So maybe just a little abstinence as a token gesture on my behalf won't go amiss."

Megan laughed. "You're such a martyr."

"Not really. I'm happy if I'm with you and you're happy." He pulled her close, settling her face against his neck.

Megan wrapped her left leg with one of his and pressed her hand over his heart. It was beating steadily.

"Okay, but tomorrow night, Mr Carter, I expect a full service."

He chuckled. "Oh, don't you worry about that, it's definitely on the menu."

Megan smiled and shut her eyes. She was tired. The emotions of the day had taken their toll—seeing her parents and sister, the dress, the news about her family moving to America, and of course all the excitement of having Georgie and Tom over, too, and the last-minute wedding preparations.

Soon she was aware of her body sinking into slumber. Her thoughts began to drift and become disjointed.

Her brain came up with a tangle of images.

The cresting waves and the golden sand on the beach. Her dress, all pretty and white and floating around her body.

She thought of the orchid bouquet she'd ordered—the tiny

flowers so delicate – and in her dream they were dotted into her hair as well.

The church rose before her. The one she'd been all set to marry Dylan in. Except this one wasn't surrounded by the graveyard. Instead, waves splashed against it and children's sandcastles were built by the arched doorway.

Her father was there in his suit, smiling at her, his eyes glazed with emotion. She loved him so much. Her father had always been there for her. No matter what.

He held out his hand and she walked towards him with her toes sinking into the warm sand.

A calmness came over her as she looked into the shadows of the church. Georgie was there, so was Olivia, and her mother. They were smiling, urging her to come in.

She stepped into the aisle. Now she was wearing her shoes. They were so high, too high, she was towering and tall, wobbly as well. Could she do it? Would she be able to walk to the altar and get married this time?

She continued forwards. There were cobbles on the floor of the church – she was worried she'd slip, or turn her ankle.

A glance down told her there were more than cobbles there. Dark shadowed hands reached upwards, fingers outstretched.

Terror washed through her. Nausea gripped her. A sense of panic shot into her system.

Frantically, she looked around, searching for James.

She saw Brendon and he gave her a thumbs-up sign. Couldn't he see the carpet of devil's hands that were grappling for her heels, her feet, her ankles?

A shout, a cry for help caught in her throat. Her father was gone, his place taken by her mother.

She was confused. What was happening? Where was James?

"Megan."

His voice cut through her confusion and fear.

There he was. Standing at the end of the aisle, smiling at her. He was tall and broad and so handsome in his suit. He held out his hands to her, waiting for her.

She mustered her courage, kicked at the hands trying to keep her from him, and walked with her chin held high. It was frightening, knowing what was beneath her. What darkness could claim her.

But James was a beacon of light and hope and love. On and on she walked, and with each step her nerves calmed, the shoes were easier to walk in now and the hands faded into the distance.

"Megan." He took her hands.

"James." She looked up into his eyes. Eyes she wanted to be able to look into for all time.

He said her name again and again, stroked her hair and drew her close.

She stifled a sob, but it wasn't one of sadness – it was one of happiness. She'd fought her demons, chosen her path and the shoes she wanted to walk that path in, and had been led to James. The man she would soon call her husband. His presence made her feel safe and secure, happy and loved.

She tried to tell him this but the words were thick in her throat, stuck on her tongue.

"Megan."

"Mmm…"

"Megan, wake up."

She blinked open her eyes and stared at the ceiling and the pale moonlight shadows dappled over it.

"Megan, are you okay?" James lifted her chin so she was looking at him.

"Yes." She nodded and drew a deep breath.

"Were you dreaming?" he asked.

"Yes." She thought back to the images that had played in her mind as she'd slept.

"Was it a nightmare?" He seemed concerned.

"It started off that way, but not by the end."

"Oh, I see. What was it about?"

"A recurring dream I've had for a while now. But this time it ended differently."

"And that's a good thing?"

"Yes. I get the feeling it won't be back." She closed her eyes and snuggled against him. "I've come out the other side of that one."

19

Megan stood in the bedroom, the sea breeze gliding around her, and studied her reflection. It was the second time she'd been dressed as a bride yet now, today, it felt so very different. Preparing to become Mrs Carter was natural. Her soul was sure. Her heart beat in time with James'.

Their baby grew in her womb.

She slid her hand over her stomach. She was marrying the man of her dreams and he was on the beach waiting for her. His best man, Grant, had their rings in his pocket and their closest family and friends were preparing to celebrate with them.

Next to where the ceremony would take place the waves rose, crested and fell, as rhythmic and eternal as their love for each other. There could be no better place for them to say their vows.

With a steady hand, she applied her favourite red MAC lipstick, blotted her lips together, then gave her wrists a final squirt of perfume—the sweet one she knew James particularly liked.

She was ready to go and get married.

Knock. Knock.

"Come in."

Her father peeked around the door. "Are you ready, darling?"

"Yes. This time, I really am."

"And they're all waiting for you." He smiled and stepped in. He was holding a slip of paper.

"What's that?" she asked. "It's not quite speech time yet, or were you waiting outside the door practicing?"

"No, it's not mine." He held it out.

"Oh?"

"It's for you, from James."

She took it and frowned. "He hasn't run off, has he?" She laughed and hoped the sound didn't have a nervous wobble in it.

"No. He was down on the beach, waiting by that elaborate arch of flowers Brendon was fussing with, when I left him a few minutes ago. He looks ready to get hitched even if he's not in a traditional morning suit."

"Good." She unfolded the paper. "That he looks ready to get married, that is."

She started reading.

Glitter

I know you have a habit of running away in those fancy shoes of yours, so I thought it best to remind you. Today you're only running one way, and that's towards me.

I can't wait to call you my wife. I love you so much.

J X

Megan read the note twice. Her eyes stung a little and she blinked rapidly, hoping not to wreck her eye makeup. It was true—she was a runner. She'd run from Dylan and James.

But not today. Today she'd walk steady and proud the way she had in her dream last night. She was sure of her love, of his love for her and the commitment she was making for the rest of her life.

She opened her jewellery box and carefully placed the note inside. She'd keep it forever.

"Everything okay?" her dad asked, a worried crease lining his brow.

"Yes, fine. All fine." She smiled.

"Well, let's go then." He stepped up to her and kissed her cheek. "You look radiant, glowing. It's going to be wonderful living near enough to get to know James better and, of course, our beautiful grandchild."

She raised her eyebrows. "What? Living nearer?"

"Oh, don't pretend you don't know." He chuckled. "Your mother and Olivia are terrible at keeping secrets, so a secret about a secret is a lost cause. They could barely contain themselves in the cab on the way to the hotel last night. I think we maybe got one hundred yards before they blurted out that you knew."

"Oh dear. Sorry."

"Don't be sorry. Nothing could spoil how I feel today or how much I'm looking forward to the future. It's right that we'll all be living in the same country again. Living on the other side of the world from you has been hard. I don't want to do it again."

"I agree, it's been hard and I'm glad it's all changing." She gave him a hug, loving the feel of his big shoulders and the strength his embrace always gave her. There was no one like her father—he was so special to her. "And I couldn't be happier, Dad. It's worked out wonderfully and we'll all have so much fun together."

"We will." He held her at arm's-length. "Oh, and before I forget."

"What?"

He dug into his pocket and pulled out a small turquoise box with Tiffany & Co written on the top in black writing. "This is for you."

"What is it?"

"Open it and see."

She did as he'd instructed.

Nestled on the soft padding was a silver necklace with a pendant. The pendant was unusual because it was a tiny high-heeled shoe with little diamonds set in it.

"Do you like it?" he asked.

"Oh, Dad, I love it."

"We saw it and couldn't resist. It seemed so right for you."

"I'll wear it today."

"You don't have to, it's just a keepsake."

"I do. I want to. My shoe business is a big part of my life and James is so supportive of it, as are you and Mum." She carefully took the necklace from the box. "It's right that I should wear it."

He smiled and took it from her, his fingers big on the tiny clasp. "Okay. Turn around."

She did, not having to scoop up her hair because it was already pinned high.

"There we go," he said.

Megan touched the delicate shoe that sat just beneath the hollow of her throat. "Thank you."

"You're welcome. But now it's time to go down to the beach. Your groom has waited long enough."

She nodded. "He's a patient man."

"Everyone's patience has a limit. We don't want him worrying that you have cold feet."

"Definitely not cold feet."

"So you'll make it to the end of the aisle this time? Albeit a sandy one."

"Yes. I will."

He smiled and opened the door.

Georgie was hovering on the other side of it. She wore a simple pale cream dress and a string of pearls. She'd also put tiny slides set with pearls in her hair and they sat amongst her curls, which she'd carefully coifed and sprayed into position.

"Wow, Megan," she said. "The dress was gorgeous on a hanger but on you, well, it's lovely."

"Do you like it?" Megan asked, running her hand down the front, removing an invisible crease.

"It's beautiful, and ideal for a beach wedding."

"Is everything ready? Down there." Megan nodded at the balcony that held the steps leading to the beach. A flutter of nerves went through her. Not about marrying James, but the fact they had a houseful of friends and family to entertain for the day.

"All set."

"And what about in the kitchen?"

"The caterers assure me they have it all under control.

The cake is on its stand looking delicious, the champagne is chilling and the meal is being prepared."

"And the table, is it okay? We spent so long setting it but I was worried if the breeze picked up, the flowers would—"

"It's fine. The weather isn't going to change and the table is just as we left it." She turned to the dresser. "And talking of flowers, it's time for you to hold your bouquet."

Megan took the delicate twelve-stemmed bunch of white and pale lemon-coloured orchids. They were bound with glossy dark green ribbon and their tiny heads bobbed slightly as she held them before her.

"That's you all set." Georgie pressed a kiss to her cheek. "Go marry Hot Guy."

Megan giggled, a burst of sound that seemed to fill her chest. It felt like so long ago they'd all referred to James as Hot Guy. Who would have thought back then, in London, when he'd been someone she'd admired from afar, that one day she'd become his wife?

They headed through the living area and out onto the balcony. Her father wore shoes with his smart black trousers and crisp white shirt, but Megan and Georgie were bare-footed.

She glanced at the table, set with white linen and crystal and extended so everyone could enjoy the meal together with the ocean as their backdrop. More orchids had been placed in sturdy pots and a tub of silver heart confetti had been sprinkled over the tablecloth, making it sparkle in the sunlight.

It wasn't a huge hall decked out for hundreds of people. There'd be no live band and for her, no champagne, but she couldn't imagine a happier place or way to spend the first few hours after becoming Mrs Carter.

"Brendon thinks of everything," Georgie said, pointing at Megan's bridal shoes on a white satin cushion at the top of the steps next to the gate. "They're waiting for you to put on when you come up here after the ceremony."

"He's such a star." Megan smiled.

"I wonder if we'll be at another wedding before the year is out," Georgie said, starting to descend the steps.

"What do you mean?"

"Brendon and Zane. They're besotted with each other."

"Yes, that's true." Megan gripped the handrail and followed Georgie, her father close behind. "And it would be lovely for him to get his happily ever after, too. He deserves it."

"I agree. But..."

"But what?"

"He might come and live in LA, too—me and Tom will be on our own in London."

"Oh, Georgie, you won't be on your own. We'll come and visit lots, and you can come here whenever you want."

She shrugged. "Perhaps I'll have to branch out, set up an office over here. I'm sure LA needs recruitment services."

"That sounds like a solution," Megan's father said. "Then everyone can live in the sunshine by the beach."

"And talking of the beach, that's a scene from a fairy tale." Georgie gestured at the small congregation awaiting them.

An arch of white flowers sat parallel to the shoreline, the waves stopping about twenty feet from it. Linen-covered seats with pale yellow bows on the back had been set out and were now occupied by guests.

The officiator, like Megan's father, wore black trousers and a white shirt. He held a small book and was speaking to James.

Megan took a moment to study her fiancé. He'd opted for cream chinos and a linen shirt, the first couple of buttons undone. His hair was neat and he was clean-shaven. Like her, he was barefoot.

She'd never seen him more gorgeous or relaxed.

The officiator must have seen her and said as much to James, because he turned and looked directly at her just as she stepped onto the sand.

He smiled.

She returned the smile. Even from where she stood she

could see the love in his expression.

The crowd turned, too.

"Here goes," her father said, holding out the crook of his elbow.

Megan took it, and as she walked, Georgie a few paces ahead of them, she breathed in the fresh, salty air. Her heart was full of love. There wasn't a fibre in her body that screamed run. She was going to her true love. The man of her dreams.

On this sandy aisle there were no stones waiting to trip her up or turn her ankle. No mean, dark hands wanting to pull her into the depths of despair. She saw only light and happiness, safety, and a future full of laughter.

Her new mother-in-law, a gem of a lady, gave her a small wave.

She inclined her head slightly, then caught the gazes of Olivia and her mother, who were beaming.

Brendon blew her a kiss then clasped his hands beneath his chin and sighed.

Finally, she settled her attention on James again.

He stood, feet hip-width apart, arms at his sides and the breeze pressing his shirt against his torso. He was big and strong and all hers.

What more could she want in life?

As she drew level with him she studied his eyes.

"You made it," he said quietly.

"Of course."

"I'm glad."

Georgie reached for her bouquet and her father stepped away.

James took her hands and squeezed them.

"We're gathered here today," the officiator said, "to witness and celebrate the union of James Carter and Megan Winter in their marriage to one another."

His voice carried on the sound of the waves and the sun heated Megan's bare shoulders. This was so much more her than a stuffy dark church. The beach, the outdoors, it was at one with nature, where she wanted to be.

"I believe you've written your own vows?" The officiator said.

"Yes," James said. "We have."

"I'd like to invite Megan to read hers first."

"Of course."

Grant stepped forwards and handed her the sheet of paper she'd given him earlier.

"Thanks," she said, a small roll of nerves attacking her belly. Funny how she could speak on national TV but now, in front of family and friends, a frisson of apprehension was going through her. She guessed it was the enormity of the words. This wasn't gossip about fashion and shoes. These were promises of a lifelong commitment to one person.

"James," she said, glancing at the vows she'd written a few days ago to remind herself what she wanted to say. "On our special day, our wedding day, the eternal sun shines on us and the ocean dances for us. And how can it not, for our hearts beat as one and our love is stronger than forever." She paused and breathed deeply. "I promise to be a faithful, true and supportive wife from this day forward, and be kind and understanding in all life's circumstances, as we face them together. In the joys and sorrows, the good times and bad, I will always be there for you, to comfort you, love you, honour and cherish you, with my heart, body and soul for now and forevermore."

She'd spoken without taking her attention from his face, having learnt the words that had come from her heart.

He swallowed, his Adam's apple dipping, then pressed his lips together.

She passed the paper back to Grant, who then handed James his vows.

He opened them. Paused. Also seemed to gather himself with a few deep breaths.

The crowd was silent.

A wave crashed towards them then fizzed its retreat over the sand nearby. A bird called overhead and the breeze caught a lock of Megan's hair.

She pushed it behind her ear then took James' hand in hers again. "It's okay."

"I know," he said quietly.

He cleared his throat.

"Megan," he said, his voice clear and strong. "I, James Carter, on this wonderful day on this beautiful beach, affirm my love and devotion to you as I invite you to share my life. You are the most beautiful, smart and generous person I have ever known, with a bright and sparkling soul that has bonded with mine in a way I never thought possible. I promise to respect you and love you always with my heart and body. And with kindness, unselfishness and trust, I will work by your side to create a wonderful life for us and our children." He paused and smiled at her. "I take you, Megan, to be my lawful wedded wife, to have and to hold, from this day forward. To love and care for you when luck is on our side, and on the days it isn't, I give you myself for as long as we both shall live."

A tremble went through Megan as his words settled in her mind and heart. For a tough guy, he could be damn romantic at times and it always caught her out.

She steeled herself to keep her emotions in check.

It seemed he was doing the same thing and as the officiator spoke, they gazed at each other, finding strength in one another.

"Do we have the rings?"

"Yes." Grant stepped forwards, digging into the pocket of his chinos. "Here they are." He handed over a small black box.

The officiator opened them and passed one to James and one to Megan. "James, please…" He indicated to Megan.

James reached for her hand and slipped the ring to her first knuckle. "With this ring, I give you my promise that from this day forward I will give you all my love, and you shall not walk alone." He slipped the slim gold band into place.

Megan admired it, then picked out the thicker band that was for her to put on James' finger. She felt so calm. It was all so right.

She took James' hand and slotted the ring on. "This ring has no end or beginning, so shall my love for you be. As I place it on your body, I give you all that I am, and all that I shall become."

She slid it into position, enjoying the way ring sat and would show the world that he was hers—that they were a team, a solid unit that couldn't be broken.

"Under California law and the powers vested in me, I now pronounce you man and wife and you may kiss the bride," the officiator said with a broad smile.

Suddenly she was in James' arms. He held her close and pressed his lips to hers.

She sighed against her new husband and looped her hands behind his neck. Will I ever get close enough to him?

It was a moment she'd remember forever, standing on this beach, the waves and the wind and her friends and family sharing her union with the man who had become her everything.

And soon, in a few months' time, they'd be adding to their family. A perfect next chapter of their story that would take them for the ride of their lives.

20

James

Four years later

James sat by Grant in the editing suite at the LA studio and studied the screen. They were watching a final proof of a documentary about the rebuilding of New Orleans since Hurricane Katrina. The government had helped, but not enough, the locals thought. The levy was still a structural risk and required further improvement, and some of the poorest communities remained in need of basic provisions.

"What do you think, boss?" Grant asked as the final credits rolled.

"I think that's it, a wrap." James crossed his arms and nodded. "We've got everything in there we wanted to highlight, plus extra testimonials. The camera work has your usual flair, which you know I always appreciate, and the soundtrack is spot on."

"Thanks, and yes, I agree. It's taken a while but we got there in the end."

"And without getting shot at, which is always a bonus."

Grant chuckled. "Yeah, can't say I miss those days."

"You don't? Wasn't it exciting? You talked about it for months." James was surprised that Grant didn't ever suggest going to more places like Central America. He'd kept their adventures in El Salvador as a main topic of conversation for ages after they'd returned, and the entire time they'd been putting the documentary together he'd kept bringing up the moment they'd hidden behind the leaves, and the snake that had wended its way over James' shoulder and down his arm.

"Because I could talk about it, I hadn't taken a bullet in the head or chest." Grant reached for his jacket. "But it's out of my system now. And with Shannon in my life, well, let's just say I don't want to do that months away from home thing again."

"I get you there, buddy." James flicked off the screen. "I'd rather be at home than anywhere else in the world. Which reminds me, how is it going with the new house?"

"Yeah, all good. We should be in by next month, though Shannon wants to wait until we're back from honeymoon before we move in together."

"Ah, a traditional girl."

"Well, it's one of the things I like about her." Grant smiled in the lopsided way James had come to associate with Shannon.

His best friend had been a different man since meeting her the year before when attending a photography convention. The pretty wildlife photographer had captured his heart and Grant had been smitten from day one. It hadn't taken him long to propose and now a big wedding was being planned in Newport, where she was from, and they were buying a house by the beach.

James was pleased. Grant had finally said goodbye to his philandering ways and put a stop to the one-night stands that hadn't eased his loneliness.

Plus Shannon and Megan got on great, which meant fun trips out when they could all fit it into their schedules.

"So I'll catch you after the weekend," Grant said, heading out of the door.

"Yes, and thanks, for all your hard work on this one."

"We're a team." Grant smiled. "Wish me luck, I've got about fifty wedding cakes to taste tomorrow. How can they all be so different?"

"No idea." James laughed. "See you."

Grant left the editing suite and James turned to his laptop. He attended to a few emails then sent the final documentary to Rue for approval. A screening with the board would be organised. He expected it to be aired within two months. At which point he'd be immersed in his next project, which was already planned and centred around prison overcrowding in California.

He stood and reached for his car keys. He had a Mickey Mouse key ring on them, a memento of a recent trip to Disneyland.

Soon he was on the freeway. As always, the sun shone, and he expected Megan would be on the beach when he arrived home.

He smiled and flicked on the radio. He was looking forward to seeing her. They'd been apart for four days while she'd been in New York.

Winter Shoes had well and truly gone global. And with Megan already owning her own stores in London, Paris, Berlin and Milan, she now had two in the United States—one in LA and the other in New York City.

The New York City branch was the newest and she'd been attending the launch, with Brendon and Iris also in tow, of course. And naturally Charlotte had gone, too. Wherever Megan went, their daughter went. She'd tried leaving her with her mother or a nanny when she'd been away on business and Charlotte had been fine, but Megan had hated every minute of it.

When she'd called James in tears, preparing to cancel meetings to jump on the next flight home, he'd reminded her of what she'd said when pregnant—that she'd wanted to be a mother first and a businesswoman second.

So with his support, and Brendon's and her mother's, Charlotte was now becoming a little globetrotter herself.

He pulled into the driveway of their home and switched off the engine. Silence surrounded him and for a moment he sat and absorbed it. Soon his world would be full of his daughter's excited chatter and Megan's enthusiastic details of the store launch.

How different his life had become since meeting his wife. Now it was never dull, never boring. There was always light and fun in his days. He had so much love for her and Charlotte that sometimes it felt too enormous to fit in his heart. He'd do anything for them, anything at all. Give them what they needed for all eternity and fight to protect them should anyone be foolish enough to harm a hair on their heads.

Stepping out of the car into the heat, he then clicked his key fob to lock his car. Once in the house the sound of waves crashing in the distance rolled up onto the balcony, and into the living area.

He spotted Charlotte's tiny sequined shoes abandoned on the floor next to Megan's sparkly heels.

After grabbing a glass of water, he wandered outside.

Sure enough, Megan and Charlotte were at the base of the steps with a red-checked blanket spread out next to them. They appeared to be involved in building a big sandcastle that had shells balanced on the top.

He toed off his shoes then yanked at his socks. Navigating down the steps, he enjoyed seeing Megan interacting with Charlotte. As he got closer he could hear them chattering about which tower the princess would live in and where the king could keep his horses.

Charlotte was clearly into the imagination of their game and was carefully answering her mother, her soft, childish voice carrying on the breeze.

"Hi," James said, stepping onto the sand.

"Daddy!" Charlotte flung down her spade and jumped to her feet, sending a flurry of sand skittering over the castle.

She wore pink shorts and a pink T-shirt with her favourite cartoon character on the front. She also had on a tiny New York Yankees peaked cap.

James grinned and knelt down, arms stretched out.

Charlotte threw herself at him and wrapped her arms around his neck.

James stood, holding her close then spun around.

She giggled and held tighter. "Faster. Faster."

He turned some more, enjoying the feel of her tiny arms

clinging to him and how she smelled of baby shampoo.

"We'll get dizzy, we'll fall over," he said, slowing.

"I don't care. I like being dizzy."

"And how did you like New York?" he asked, flicking the peak on her cap.

"It was big and there was no beach. I like the beach. Mommy said we could build the biggest sandcastle ever when we got home and we are. Look."

She wriggled, clearly keen to get back to her game.

James set her down and she rushed for her spade then dropped to her knees to continue working on her sandcastle.

"Hey, gorgeous," James said, sitting on the blanket next to Megan.

"Hi."

She smiled and his heart melted a little more. She was so pretty, so adorable and such a wonderful mother.

Was she really his?

It seemed she was.

He leaned in for a kiss and hoped she understood how glad he was she was home. That the trip had been and gone and they had nothing but being together planned for the whole weekend.

She sighed and gripped his biceps, as though keeping him close.

"I missed you," he whispered.

"I missed you, too."

He kissed her again, enjoying her soft lips against his.

"How did it go?" he asked.

"New York is fun. Big and busy and there's always something going on and so many opportunities. And having Charlotte plus Brendon and Mum there was great, but..."

"But?"

"But I'm glad to be home."

"I'm glad to have you home. The house seems too big on my own."

"You lived alone here for years."

"Yeah, and it felt empty then. It's only been a home since you arrived." He glanced at Charlotte. "And our baby girl, of course."

"She enjoyed the zoo in Central Park. Mum took her there while I was in the shop on the first day."

"What did you see at the zoo?" James directed at Charlotte.

"I saw monkeys and bears and a snake and pen…gins." She struggled with the word penguin.

"Penguins," James corrected. "Did it have little wings?" He waggled his arms at his sides. "Like this?"

"Yes." Her eyes widened. "Just like that."

"Funny, huh?"

She nodded as though suitably impressed then returned to digging the moat around her castle.

Megan leaned in close to him, obviously content to watch Charlotte play and have a break from building a home for imaginary royalty.

James drew her near and stretched out his legs.

He breathed in the fresh sea air and enjoyed the sound of the waves and Charlotte's little song that she was singing as she dug.

"Did you get the final edits done?" Megan asked, slipping her finger between two buttons on his short-sleeved shirt. She stroked over the skin on his abdomen.

"Yes, all wrapped up and sent to Rue."

"Are you pleased with it?"

"Of course, I wouldn't have sent it off otherwise."

"True." She paused. "Will it be another award-winner, do you think?"

"I don't know."

"Another Sparkling Stars trophy would be nice. You have the ones for *Poor Choices* and *Cartel Cocaine Crisis,* so why not *When the Wind Blows,* too?"

"Nice thought."

"More than a thought, it's a possibility. How is Grant, by the way? Wedding nerves yet?"

"He's cool. I think he'll be glad when it's over. He's not

one for a big fuss, it's mainly because it's what Shannon wants that he's going along with it all." He held Megan a little tighter. "He just wants to marry her, and if he's got to taste fifty cakes and jump through a bunch of hoops to make that happen, he will."

"Ah, bless him. They're really in love, aren't they?"

"Only like we are." He reached for her hand and spread out her fingers, raised her palm to his mouth and kissed the centre.

"Do you ever regret not having a big wedding?" she asked.

"What? No, of course not." He was surprised at the question.

"Ah, that's good then."

"Why, do you?"

"No, no, not at all. The beach was the ideal spot, where you'd proposed."

"I thought so." He hesitated. "But if you'd wanted a big do, I'd have gone along with that."

"You gave me two weeks to organise it." She laughed and gently poked him with her finger.

"Only because…" He nodded at Charlotte.

"I know, I know, and it's fine. I think we have the most amazing photographs of our day. All our guests with us and the Pacific Ocean rising in the distance. Much better than the stuffy ones taken in graveyards." She shuddered. "I don't like them."

"And the meal was wonderful afterwards. So relaxing sitting on the balcony with everyone."

"I know, there wasn't an ounce of stress, just happiness."

He rested her hand down then stroked her stomach.

She wore a pale blue cotton beach dress—one that she seemed to go for when she'd been on business trips and in more formal outfits. He liked it. The shape showed off her trim waist and it was short enough for him to admire her tanned legs.

"And the last thing we wanted was you stressed," he said.

"When you were carrying Charlotte in here." He pressed her stomach slightly.

"True." She smiled. "And I wasn't stressed. Just blissfully happy. And I still am."

"Me too. In fact, on our wedding day I didn't think I could be happier but as life ticks along, I fall more and more in love with you and feel more and more content with the world and my place in it." He paused. "There's lots of bad stuff out there and I've made it my job to see it and report on it. But here, with you, in our home, it's all as it should be."

"And I don't want that to ever change." She looked up at him, her eyes sparkling.

James took a deep breath. He'd wanted to bring up something that had been on his mind for a while now. This seemed as good at time as any.

"What is it?" she asked, tipping her head and studying him. "What's going through your mind, James Carter?"

He smiled. "Well…"

"Well what?"

"How would you feel…?" He looked at where his hand rested on her lower abdomen. "About having another baby?"

"Another one?" She raised her eyebrows but her gentle smile didn't falter.

"Yes. I'm sure Charlotte would love a baby brother or sister."

"I'm sure she would."

He tried to read her expression. Did she want to go through pregnancy and childbirth again? She'd had no complications with Charlotte, everything had gone well, but still, there was nothing easy about having a baby – he'd been there, he'd seen what hard work it was.

"I think it's a lovely idea," she said, stroking his cheek.

"You do?"

"Yes, it's been on my mind, too."

Contentment mixed with excitement collided inside his

soul – another baby, his and Megan's child, adding to their family. What could be more perfect?

"And," Megan said, placing her lips by his ear, "it's time for Charlotte's nap, she's jet lagged from our trip and could do with a rest before dinner, so…" She paused. "Maybe we could start trying right now."

He slipped his fingers into her hair and spoke onto her lips. "I like the way you think, Glitter."

Sparkling Stilettos

Excerpt

Chapter One

Megan

"Oh my goodness, darling, you look fabulous. Utterly… totally…bloody fabulous."

Megan held her full champagne flute to Brendon's and they chinked rims, the sound tinkling around the plush West London hotel room.

"Thank you," she said then hesitated with the glass by her lips. She stared in the mirror at her unfamiliar bridal reflection. With her dark hair piled high, her makeup natural and long, dangling silver earrings, she hardly recognised herself. "But do you think it's maybe a bit over the top, you know, with the tiara?"

"No, no, not at all," Brendon said, shoving his hand on his waist and jutting out his left hip. "You, my beauty, are a princess, so of course you should be wearing a bejewelled crown." He tutted and tapped the base of her stem. "Sup, sup, it's your wedding day, champers needs to be drunk from dawn till dusk."

"Yes, but not too much," Georgie said with a smile but also a hint of sternness in her tone. "We don't want you sloshed as you walk down the aisle, Megan. You've got towering heels to keep control of. Beautiful, bespoke heels yes, I agree, but still, they're high even for you."

Megan took a deep breath and curled her toes into the soft beige carpet—her feet were a little cold even though the room was warm. In one hour she would be wearing the stunning new heels she'd designed and walking down the aisle to marry Dylan Dunkin-Buckshaw—yes, she would be Mrs Megan Rose Dunkin-Buckshaw and damn proud to be.

She could live with the name. Of course she could. She'd be sad to say goodbye to Winter, though, because Megan Rose Winter had a nice ring to it. But she'd used the name Winter to set up her beloved shoe design business a few years before, so if she looked at it like that, she wasn't really giving up her name. She'd still have it, and still use it on a daily basis. The only difference would be that her driving licence and bank account would say Dunkin-Buckshaw. But what did that matter? Who ever saw a person's licence or bank account? Well, Dylan would see her bank account now. He'd said they'd pool their cash once married—apparently that was what couples did after tying the knot.

"Are you sure you're not going for the red?" Brendon held up her scarlet MAC lipstick. It was her favourite, the only one she wore. But today she'd decided not to. Today she was going for nude gloss.

"No." She shook her head. "Dylan doesn't really like it. He says it's…" She paused, remembering the conversation.

"What?" Georgie fussed with a tendril of Megan's hair that had escaped. "What does he say?"

"Yes, tell us?" Brendon added with a frown. "I'm curious

now."

"He thinks it's a bit tarty."

Georgie gasped and shook her head. "No!"

Brendon slapped his hand over his mouth and widened his eyes.

"He said that?" Georgie asked. "He actually, really and truly said that?"

Megan shrugged. It was no big deal. He was entitled to have an opinion.

"But you've worn that shade for years." Brendon tutted. "It's so…you. It's your signature lippy."

"And it suits you so well, highlights the pretty shape of your mouth," Georgie added.

"Thank you, but it's just for today."

"Are you sure?" Brendon asked. "Because if you never wear it again I'll be heartbroken. In fact, I may as well just lie down here right now and die." He gestured to the four-poster bed then made a show of falling back onto it. He threw his arms over his face. "Oh, goodbye to the scarlet lips that we know and love. How can I go on?"

"Don't be so dramatic, it's only lipstick." Megan laughed. "Come on. Help me with the dress."

Georgie glanced at her iPhone. "Yes, you should get dressed. Time is ticking away. The bells will soon be ringing."

Megan stood. Her stomach was heavy even though she hadn't been able to eat that morning. Nerves, most likely. This was, after all, the biggest day of her life—or so she'd been told. If she wasn't nervous there'd be something wrong with her, right? If there were no butterflies swarming she'd be abnormal. Every bride had this sensation, she'd read about it, seen it in movies.

"How does this feel?" Georgie asked, adjusting the ties on the back of the white basque Megan wore. "Too tight?"

"No it's fine. It kind of feels like it's holding me together." Megan huffed at her silliness but it was the truth. With all the emotions rolling about inside her—apprehension, excitement, awestruck—the basque was like wearing a hug. It was comforting and made her feel secure.

"Your new husband will love that later," Brendon said, crawling off the bed and nodding approvingly. His gaze took in Megan standing in her sexy underwear. "My, my, if I wasn't into men, my sweetpea, I'd do you."

"Well thanks, I think." Megan giggled and reached for a pack of unopened white stockings.

"Who are you kidding, Brendon?" Georgie said, before picking up her champagne and taking a sip. "I shouldn't think you've got the energy for any of that after last weekend."

"Last weekend was a business trip." Brendon scowled.

"Hah, business, yes, if you're in the business." Georgie rolled her eyes. "Everyone knows that you and Timothy Hung-like-a-Donkey Curtis weren't interested in checking out that hotel in Brighton for a possible gig, you were just on a shagathon trip."

"Well, I take great offence to that, Georgie Porgy Pudding and Pie, because actually that's exactly what we did. Prada is looking at holding a launch party there for their new line of summer purses"

"Yes, we'll believe it when we see it." Georgie laughed and set down her glass.

Normally Megan's ears would have pricked at the mention of Prada summer purses—she loved purses for all seasons and all occasions—but not today.

"You want me to do that, Megan?"

"No, I can manage." The wrapper on the stocking box was proving tricky and her hands were a little shaky.

"Here." Georgie took the package and deftly opened it.

"Thanks." Megan smiled. She was so happy that her two best friends were with her today. She couldn't have done it without them. They were her rocks, her pillars of support, her port in a storm. They'd met over five years ago at a mutual friend's party, all newly single and all wanting to have some fun. Before long they'd been partying hard, but also kicking back and putting the world to rights together. Now they spoke or dropped in on each other most days, did lunch or met for cocktails every week, and tried to get away at least once each summer to worship the sun on some tropical beach.

"Don't look so worried," Georgie said with a slight frown.

"Yeah, are you okay?" Brendon asked.

"I'm fine, absolutely fine." Megan took a deep breath. "Come on, let's get this show on the road." She gathered the first stocking and carefully fed her right foot into it then pulled it up to her thigh. She repeated the action with her left and smoothed the lace holdup trims to ensure there were no creases.

"Ah, ah, one more thing before the dress." Georgie dipped into her handbag. "Here."

"A garter?" Megan queried. "Really? Isn't that kind of old-fashioned?"

"Of course it's old-fashioned, it's traditional." Brendon nodded seriously. "Something old, something new, something borrowed, something blue."

"Yes, you have to wear one. It would be bad luck otherwise." Georgie sank to her knees at Megan's feet, garter held into a wide 'O'. She smiled up at Megan. "The tiara is old, the dress is new and this is something borrowed and…" She twisted the garter to show off a tiny blue bow. "Is also blue."

"Oh, okay." Megan giggled at how serious her friends were taking this tradition. What was going to happen if she didn't have something old, new, borrowed and blue? It would hardly spoil the day or curse their marriage for all of time.

Would it?

Georgie slipped the garter up Megan's leg to her thigh.

Megan stroked her finger over the delicate white trim. It was very pretty and no doubt Dylan would enjoy removing it when they reached the bridal suite—possibly with his teeth.

"This dress is to die for," Brendon said, holding up Megan's voluminous gown. "All this taffeta, it's enough to sink a battleship."

"Yes, I'll certainly have to navigate carefully through doorways today," Megan said then took a sip of champagne. She set the glass aside. "Come on then, help me into the monster." She laughed.

Georgie didn't laugh with her, instead she sighed and clasped her hands under her chin.

"You okay, Georgie?" Megan asked.

"Yes, of course. I'm just so happy for you and that this day has finally come. We've all talked for years about who would be first to get hitched and now it's happening."

Megan reached for her hand and squeezed. "It will happen for you and Tom soon, I'm sure it will."

Georgie and Tom had been together for over a year and things were getting serious. They'd skied at Christmas, met the parents and both had a drawer at each other's apartment for spare clothes and toiletries—surely a sign of true commitment.

Megan shrugged. "Maybe, maybe not, but it doesn't matter today. Today is all about you and Dylan."

"Who is likely to be arriving at church with his best man as we speak," Brendon said, before clicking his tongue on the roof of his mouth. "There is an expectant groom waiting, so chop, chop ladies. Enough of this chatter, you two could talk for England."

"And you couldn't?" Georgie grinned.

It took both her friends to assist Megan into her dress. Luckily she could step into it, which meant her hair and makeup weren't in danger, but still, the sheer amount of material created quite a challenge.

Brendon fussed over the many hems, straightening the layers and fluffing it out so the periphery was even bigger. Georgie fiddled with the top, drawing up the side zipper and puffing the cupped silk sleeves.

"It's so beautiful," Georgie said wistfully.

"And so virginal," Brendon said, then cackled. "Except we know that's not true."

Megan skimmed her palms over the tight material at her waist then over her hips. Her hands became lost in the meringue nest of taffeta. "I've had some fun but I have standards." She rolled her eyes. "But not as much fun as you, Brendon."

"Yeah, well, I've not finished having fun yet," he said, standing. "There's many more fish out there for me to reel in and have my wicked way with."

"But don't you want to find the one?" Georgie asked, helping herself to a squirt of Megan's perfume.

"Yes of course, but not for a while. I've still got things I want to do, places to go, people to meet. I'm not ready to commit to one person, and besides, I wouldn't know if it was the right person anyway."

"What do you mean?" Megan asked, taking her perfume from Georgie and spritzing it over her neck and onto her wrists.

"Well, I don't know how you do it." He looked between them. "How you can be so sure you've met your soulmate? The man you're meant to be with for all of time. Go to bed with each night and wake up each morning next to."

"You'll just know," Georgie said.

"But how?" Brendon held up his palms. "How? Enlighten me."

"When you count the hours till you're going to see them again," Georgie said. "Think of them when planning what to eat that night so you know they'll enjoy it. Watch boring old war documentaries because that's their thing and not mind in the least because you're snuggled up on the sofa next to them. That's how you know."

Megan studied her friend. Georgie lit up when she talked of Tom. He'd captured her heart in a way no other man had. She'd never seen her so happy, so full of life—even the asthma that had always plagued her seemed to have settled. It was as if Tom's presence in her life was a soothing energy, a balm for her nerves. Megan hoped Tom would pop the question soon. It would feel so right to see Georgie in an elegant white gown walking down the aisle.

The door to the hotel room opened. Megan's mother, Iris, walked in carrying Gucci, who barked and wriggled as soon as he saw Brendon.

"Baby boy," Brendon said, rushing to pluck his tiny Pomeranian from Iris' arms. Gucci's little pink tongue rushed out to lick his master's chin and his tail waggled to a rapid tempo.

"Oh, Rose, my beautiful English Rose," Iris said, halting in her tracks as soon as she saw Megan. Her eyes misted and she pressed her lips together.

"Mum, you promised not to cry," Megan said, knowing that her mother would. She only ever called her Rose when she was feeling sentimental, and since she'd moved to Australia three years ago, she was more sentimental than ever when the family got together.

"I can't help it," Iris said. "My little girl all grown up and getting married."

"Yes, it seems that way." Megan smiled and fluffed the tulle on her dress. "What do you think?"

"I think you look beautiful. Dylan is lucky to have you. Very lucky indeed."

"Here, here to that." Georgie nodded.

"Abso-bloody-lutely," Brendon said, slipping a tiny doggie tuxedo over Gucci's head. It had a small bow tie beneath the chin, an embroidered waistcoat and tails that hung either side of Gucci's…tail.

Megan walked over to her mother and, stretching over the width of the dress, hugged her.

"No, no, please don't let me mess you up," Iris said, sniffing delicately.

"You won't mess me up, Mum, it's all fine." Megan placed a soft kiss on her mother's cheek. She smelt of lavender, as usual, and her skin was soft as satin.

"Oh, but I might." Iris gave Megan a frantic squeeze

then pulled away. "And you look so perfect. It all looks so perfect." She gestured at the door. "I've checked the cake and it's fabulous, exactly how Dylan wanted, a cascade of sparkling roses from the top tier to the base. The flowers are beautiful too, at the entrance to the reception room. The sweetest shade of baby pink and more gypsophila than you could shake a stick at."

"Good, that's good," Brendon said. "Flowers and cake are important."

"Where's Olivia?" Megan asked, wondering where her sister was. Olivia was her third bridesmaid.

"She's downstairs, with your father."

"I bet she looks beautiful." Megan adored how her bridesmaid dress complimented her sister's colouring. "What about Dad? Is he okay?" Megan asked, reaching for a tissue. She passed it to her mother, who instantly started checking her mascara hadn't run.

"He's fine with your sister, she's keeping an eye on him. She's good like that. You know, at calming him when he gets anxious."

"Yes, Olivia's great with him. But why's he anxious?" Megan hated seeing her father nervous. He was an all-round great guy, her rock, and as she'd grown from child to adult their relationship had only deepened. She loved him with all her heart.

"He's about to give away his eldest daughter, of course he's anxious. He's not so keen on giving away something so precious to him." Iris laughed but it held a note of tension. "And you most certainly are precious to him, Rose."

"Maybe he should look at it like he's gaining a son rather than giving away a daughter," Brendon said, ruffling Gucci's forehead so his fudge-coloured curls stood upright.

"I suppose," Iris said, sucking in a deep breath. "Yes, maybe that's how to look at it."

Megan studied her. She looked worried. Likely because Dad was stressed, even though he needn't be, he only had to walk a few steps down the aisle—not that she wouldn't be glad of his arm. Georgie was right, those heels, while stunning and one of her best designs yet, were hard to negotiate.

"Can you do me up?" Georgie asked, stepping in front of Megan. She'd pulled on her baby pink bridesmaid dress but the back zip was awkward for her to reach.

Megan slid it up. Georgie's hourglass frame suited the figure-hugging style perfectly and reminded her of a Marilyn Monroe photograph she'd seen once. Not least because Georgie's bubbles of blonde hair had just been cropped to jaw-length.

"Oh, Georgie," Iris said, "that dress is amazing on you. The colour is gorgeous with your skin tone and your eyes... simply stunning."

"Thank you," she said, turning back to Iris. "I'm glad Megan didn't pick lime green, I couldn't have pulled that off."

"I bet you could have worked lime green perfectly well." Megan laughed, though it was slightly forced because underneath Georgie's smile she knew there was a hint of longing. She wanted what Megan was about to have, a husband. But it would come soon, she was sure of it. Tom would eventually get around to it and bag the best thing that had ever happened to him.

"What about us?" Brendon said, striding in front of the mirror.

Gucci ran around his ankles, yapping as usual and hoping to be picked up again.

"How do we look?"

"Like the handsomest, gayest bridesmaid ever," Georgie said then laughed.

Megan reached to tickle Gucci beneath his chin but he wouldn't stay still for long enough, and besides, she could hardly reach him because of the dress. "And the handsomest doggie bridesmaid ever."

"Yes, I think we'll do." Brendon snapped down the pink satin waistcoat he wore beneath his morning suit. He then straightened the rose buttonhole. He looked good and he knew it. He even twirled around to check out his bum in the neat black trousers he wore, flicking up the tails of his morning coat to be sure.

"But we really should get going," Georgie said, again worrying about the time. "I know it's only a few minutes to the church from here but still, it's only ten minutes until the ceremony is due to start."

"Really?" Megan glanced at the clock that sat on the bedside table. Georgie was right. It was time to go.

It was time to go and get married.

And become Mrs Dunkin-Buckshaw.

Forever.

Her stomach clenched, the corset seeming to pull her muscles in even more.

Mr and Mrs Dylan Dunkin-Buckshaw.

The nerve endings in her scalp and at the base of her neck tingled. Maybe she should take Brendon's advice to her mother and look at it as not losing her name but gaining another family. There was Dylan's brother, his father and of course, his mother.

His mother. Rita. Who had been so excited about the wedding that Megan had actually stopped taking her calls in the final stages of preparation—not to be cruel, it was just too much. Her squeaky voice and over enthusiasm was draining, and Megan needed some energy left for the big day.

She'd called her yesterday, though, had bitten the bullet and picked up the phone. As she'd expected, it had been an hour of hysteria that had ranged from wild excitement to desperate despair because the napkins weren't the right shade of baby pink—how many shades of baby pink could there be?

"You okay, sweetpea?" Brendon took Megan's left hand.

"Yes, I think so." She looked at her hand in his. Her ring finger was bare, not even an indent. She'd hardly worn her engagement ring over the last six months, she'd been too worried about it getting wrecked at work with the glue she used on her designs. Now the ring was transferred to her right hand so that the new wedding band could be easily slipped on.

"You sure?" Georgie asked.

Megan pulled in as deep a breath as she could with the corset on. Her breasts pushed against the bones and she was aware of her heart thumping faster than normal.

"What is it?" Brendon asked.

"Nothing, nothing at all. I'm fine." Megan forced her mouth to turn up at the corners. "Really, let's get this show on the road."

"I'll see you there," her mother said. "Georgie and Brendon are very capable bridesmaids."

"And Gucci," Brendon added.

"And Gucci." Iris reached down and patted Gucci on the head. He licked her hand then ran excitedly in a circle.

"Yep, see you there, Mum," Megan said.

And next time we speak I'll be married.

"If I don't get the chance to say this to you later, Rose," her mother said, "know that I only ever want what is best for you. You make me so proud in everything you do, not least because you're a woman who knows what you want and you're not afraid to take it."

Megan felt her eyes tingle and her throat thicken. Tears were threatening.

A woman who knows what she wants and takes it.

More books from Totally Bound Publishing

When life hands you lemons, the right guy needs to be there to make the lemonade.

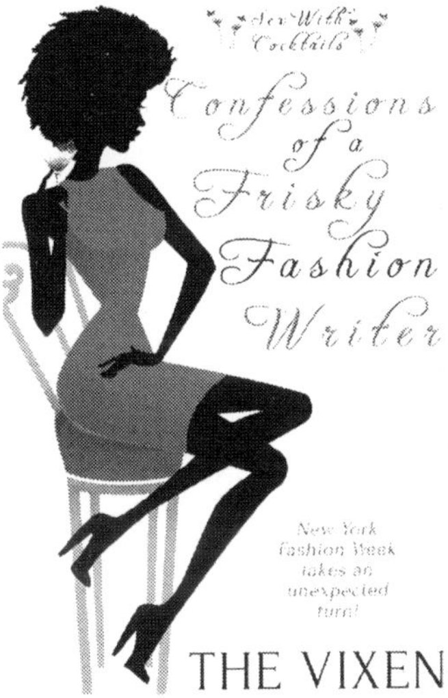

A girls' night out during New York Fashion Week takes an unexpected turn when a dashing gentleman enters the scene.

About the Author

Jess Wright

Jessica Wright shot to fame in 2010 when she first appeared in the flagship ITV2 show The Only Way Is Essex. Jessica is one of the most loved and talked about stars in the UK. Jessica has proven her popularity with the nation by carving out a fashion career with her own e-commerce site and highly successful range at Lipstick Boutique. 2015 saw Jessica launching a career as a fiction author and releasing her first novel.

Jessica has 1.5 million followers on Twitter and 1.1 million followers on Instagram.

Jess Wright loves to hear from readers. You can find contact information, website details and an author profile page at https://www.totallybound.com/

25334053R00132

Printed in Poland
by Amazon Fulfillment
Poland Sp. z o.o., Wrocław